Chasing at the Surface

a novel

by Sharon Mentyka

WESTWINDS
PRESS®

Library of Congress Cataloging-in-Publication Data
Names: Mentyka, Sharon.
Title: Chasing at the surface : a novel / by Sharon Mentyka.
Description: Portland, Oregon : WestWinds Press, [2016] | Summary: In 1997, twelve-year-old Marisa Gage retreats into her shell when nineteen orcas, mothers and new calves, become trapped in an inlet near her home soon after Marisa's whale-loving mother inexplicably left.
Identifiers: LCCN 2016013250 | ISBN 9781943328604 (pbk.)
Subjects: | CYAC: Whales—Fiction. | Mothers and daughters—Fiction. | Interpersonal relations—Fiction. | Family life—Washington (State)—Fiction. | Washington (State)—Fiction.
Classification: LCC PZ7.M53155 Ch 2016 | DDC [Fic]—dc23 LC record available at https://lccn.loc.gov/2016013250

Front cover images: top, girl with binoculars: © iStock/SashaFoxWalters; top, under the sea surface: © iStock/John Shepherd; bottom, orca: © iStock/Jon Helgason.

Edited by Michelle McCann
Designed by Vicki Knapton

Published by WestWinds Press®
An imprint of

GRAPHIC ARTS
BOOKS®
P.O. Box 56118
Portland, Oregon 97238-6118
503-254-5591
www.graphicartsbooks.com

For my family,
who forever encouraged me to chase my dream

"How inappropriate to call this planet *Earth*, when it is clearly *Ocean*."

—Arthur C. Clarke

L-25 Sub-pod

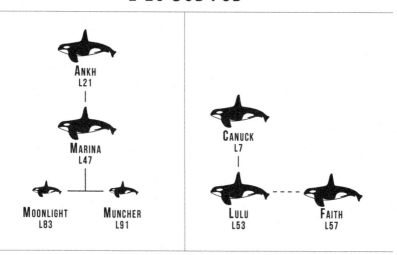

ANKH
L21

MARINA
L47

MOONLIGHT
L83

MUNCHER
L91

CANUCK
L7

LULU
L53

FAITH
L57

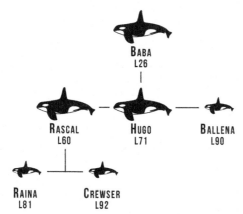

BABA
L26

RASCAL
L60

HUGO
L71

BALLENA
L90

RAINA
L81

CREWSER
L92

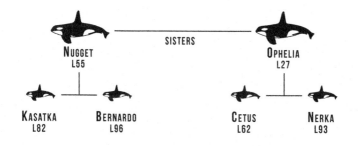

SISTERS

NUGGET
L55

OPHELIA
L27

KASATKA
L82

BERNARDO
L96

CETUS
L62

NERKA
L93

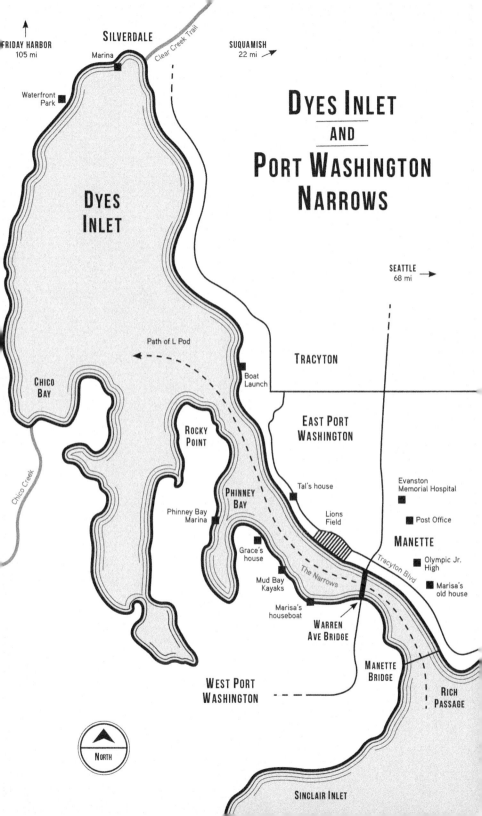

Some people thought they lost their way, others that they were chasing chum salmon. Whatever people said, looking back on it now, I know the whales came to Dyes Inlet for one reason—to help me.

It happened in October, when I was twelve years old. Nineteen killer whales came swimming into the inlet just like it was their home, except it wasn't. The whole town went crazy, caught up in the excitement of having whales as neighbors.

The problem was they arrived not long after my mother packed up and left, slipping out in the night as quietly as the pod slipped in, so whale watching wasn't exactly my priority right then. It took me a whole lot longer than most folks here in Port Washington to care about getting them home, but once I did, I couldn't seem to stop.

And that changed everything.

Because without the whales, I would've been the one who was lost.

CHAPTER 1

Orca Day 1, October, 1997

The cool early morning air blowing across the inlet carries a sharp, tangy smell that pricks at my nostrils. I lean over the side of the boat and peer down. Below, the water swirls with tails, fins, and churning froth. I dip my hand in and drag it along the surface. It's numbingly cold, just the way the fish like it.

It's salmon season here in Dyes Inlet and the chum are running strong, hundreds of fish heading upstream to the creeks for their fall spawning. When you grow up on the shores of one of the watery fingers stretching out from Puget Sound, following the run becomes a yearly ritual. Good news if you like fishing for salmon. Bad if you're bothered by the stink of the ones that die along the way.

A spray of cold saltwater hits my back. I watch as my best friend, Lena, ties off her line and hauls a hefty salmon into our boat. Her long hair covers her face as she works, lifting the fifteen-pound fish like it weighs nothing.

"It's almost too easy," she laughs. "They're everywhere!"

The chum's silvery shape, with its brilliant red and green stripes, flashes by as she *thunks* it down onto the deck. It flaps around my feet, mouth opening and closing, until finally it shudders and quiets.

Alongside, the water ripples and another wriggles by close enough for me to reach out and touch. "Marisa . . . grab it!" Lena shouts, pointing.

I lean over to make a feeble attempt and miss. "Too bad," I say, settling back in the boat. "More for you, I guess."

Lena gives me a look. We've been fishing together too long. She *knows* I can do this.

I ignore her. My heart's not into catching fish right now and it's a relief not to pretend. Instead, I close my eyes and try to relax, letting the splashing sound of fish traveling upstream fill my ears. Pretty soon our rowboat starts to rock and I hear Lena flip her line into the water again. Chum won't chase a lure, but with dozens of them passing by every minute, it doesn't matter. During salmon season, the slow sport of fishing becomes a chase.

When I glance up and across the water, I spot a long line of black boats, cruising toward the small bay at the mouth of Chico Creek. But . . . something's not right; they're traveling way too fast. Reaching for my pack, I rummage around for the binoculars.

"Uh . . . this doesn't make sense," I whisper, peering through the lenses.

"What?" Lena swivels around to look.

I blink and try to focus. I check again and a strange queasy feeling starts crawling around inside my stomach.

Whales shouldn't be *here*, not in an enclosed inlet.

"Marisa?"

"Those aren't boats out there," I tell her. "They're orcas. . . ."

"What? No way!" Lena grabs for the binoculars and scans across the water. "Oh my gosh, you're right! There must be a dozen . . . no, more. Hey," she whispers, leaning in close, "let's chase after them."

"*Chase* them?"

"Yeah, why not? C'mon, when was the last time you saw this many killer whales?"

And in a flash, she's off and running with one of her crazy ideas.

The last time I saw killer whales? Hmmm, good question.

Mom had tried to plan our annual summer trip to see the whales. But I kept putting her off. Since she left, I've racked my brain, trying to remember what I was doing then that seemed more important.

I straighten up and shake my head no. But before I can protest, Lena lowers her oars into the water again and starts rowing—fast, with big sweeping strokes. The sudden movement makes my stomach feel worse. Quickly, she maneuvers our boat a full 180 degrees, and next thing, we're headed straight toward the pod.

"Wait . . . Lena . . . no. . . ."

She really means to chase them, and she's a good enough fisherwoman to do it.

"Calm down," she laughs, not bothering to even glance my way. "I can do this."

I stay rooted to my seat and try to focus on the pile of dead salmon lying in the bottom of the boat. Lena's rowing hard now, trying to move us across the inlet to reach the swimming whales. But the October wind is strong and our little rowboat's not made for racing.

"C'mon!" she yells. "Get over here and help!"

For half a second, I consider grabbing the oars and starting to row, but in the opposite direction—*away* from the whales and back to shore. But I don't. Instead, I grip the sides of the boat and watch, frozen in place. We're almost three-quarters across the width of the inlet now and the water is eerily quiet. The whales are all bunched up now near the western shoreline. Even from forty feet away, I can see babies tucked in close to their mothers, the group packed so tightly together they form a solid line, making it hard to see where one whale stops and another begins.

Lena stops rowing. As we watch, the pod begins to dive and surface, one by one. Each time one whale comes up it faces a different direction. The biggest sends a great plume of water up into the air—*pfoosh*—and I feel the cool mist rain down on my face.

Suddenly, dangerously close, two whales breach, jumping high up from the water's surface. Our little boat pitches and rocks.

"Whoaa!" Lena yells, laughing.

But I'm not paying attention. Because as the water settles the smaller of the two whales has risen to the surface, his flank facing me. Our eyes lock. A chill runs through me and I shiver. Looking into his round, black eye feels like falling backward, into the deepest water, the most hidden place inside me.

"Marisa? You okay?"

I can't answer. It's like I'm hypnotized by that eye. Then, just before the little whale slips deeper under the water, I see it—a round spot of black just above the white patch encircling his eye. I know that marking. But . . . it couldn't be. What are the chances he'd be here now, with Mom gone?

I panic and force myself to look away from the churning water. Crawling forward, I fumble to get the oars in position, banging them against the side of the boat.

"Let's go . . . *now*," I tell Lena.

"Wait. . . ." she says, distracted. "I think they're breaking up."

I can feel her indecision. She doesn't want to let them go. I stand halfway up, but she puts one hand up to stop me.

"No, forget it. Sit," she orders, her voice quiet with disappointment. "They must be heading out."

Grabbing the oars, she guides them back into the oarlocks. A long minute passes, then she shakes her head. "I don't get it, Marisa." She flicks her wet hair back over her shoulders. "I thought you were so hot on these whales."

She wouldn't get it, of course. She doesn't remember the connection. I open my mouth, but have no clue where or how to begin. I just shake my head.

"Yeah, yeah, I know, you'll explain later. It's always *later.*"

We sit in silence, seesawing on the settling water, until finally Lena reaches for the oars. I realize I've been holding my breath and now, I allow myself to finally exhale. My body tingles as fresh blood rushes in. I'm still trying to shake off the eerie sensation I felt, staring into the whale's eye. I'm suddenly mad at myself for freezing like that, not paying closer attention to his other markings, to be really sure.

"Too bad," I hear Lena say, "we probably could have caught up with at least some of them before they left. Don't you think?" Her voice is wistful.

Two months ago, I would have agreed. Now, I've learned you can't stop anybody from leaving, not if they really want to go. As Lena maneuvers our boat smoothly back to shore, it dawns on me that there is something that would have kept Mom here in the inlet, kept her home.

The whales. I'm sure of it.

If only they decided to visit before she left.

CHAPTER 2

By the time we haul our rowboat up onto the gravel beach at the Tracyton launch, a crowd is already gathered there, buzzing about the whale sighting. I steady myself as we walk up the concrete ramp, then hang back while Lena stows our gear.

Dyes Inlet is narrow here—it's easy to see clear across to the other side where the Olympic Mountains rise up behind the tree line. Little towns sit scattered all along the shore but Tracyton is the one with the killer views. It only takes me a second to spot a few whales again, swimming just off the far shore. Plumes of water rise up off the surface as they blow.

Nearby, a couple of boats are already prepping to head out.

"Whoa!" one guy yells to his buddies. "One just came clear out of the water and rolled back down on his side."

"It's called *breaching*," I mumble, turning my back to the inlet. I can't stop wondering. Could it really have been him, our whale, here in the inlet? Maybe I'm just missing Mom so much, I imagined it.

". . . the salmon were schooled up in the shallows," I hear Lena explaining. "Maybe that's where the orcas were headed."

The crowd is growing larger by the minute.

"How close did you get?" someone asks.

"We could see them fine from where we were," I say quickly.

"Kids have more smarts than you," another man says and they all laugh.

Lena gives me a look, then smiles. I fake a smile back.

We walk in silence up the steep incline and pull our bikes out from behind the bushes. In the narrow street, the flow of people streaming down to see the whales is so thick we have to weave back and forth, back and forth, to avoid them. Just like salmon, swimming upstream.

———

Once we're past the crowd, we split up and I ride home fast, my legs pumping hard on the pedals, my head swirling with everything that's just happened. Lena might be way more easygoing than me, but in all the ways that matter, we're alike. We think about and care about the same things. Meeting her was one of the luckiest things that ever happened to me. But since Mom left—it's like there's this wall between us. My life totally changed and hers stayed the same. Talking about even the simplest things feels hard now.

I make the slow turn into the marina. The sharp smell of the inlet hits me and I remember again first visiting here almost five months ago, when school let out for the summer. Dad had heard about a houseboat that might be coming available and he wanted to check it out, "just for fun."

Dad loves Dyes Inlet. More than loves it really, he lives in awe of it. So we all took a walk here one evening, over from the house we rented on East Sixteenth Street. I didn't think much about it at the time. I was busy planning my three-month stretch of freedom that lay ahead. I sure never thought that the marina would wind up being my new "home."

Then two months later Mom left, and we actually moved, like it had all been planned. I was so angry I didn't speak to Dad for a week after.

I can remember exactly when everything started to change. It was just before school started up again in September, about a week before Mom's birthday. We'd spent the day fishing on the inlet but it was a disaster. Dad had tried a million ways, trying to get Mom to talk or even just smile at one of his jokes. Nothing had worked.

That night, I couldn't fall asleep. It was late and I'd made it halfway down the stairs when I heard them in the kitchen, talking. Dad's voice was muffled; I couldn't make out his words. At first I thought it was because he was afraid of waking me, until I heard Mom.

"Danny, don't. It's not your fault. Oh, Danno. Honey, it'll be okay."

I crouched there on the stairs, waiting for Dad to answer. Instead, the sounds coming from him got louder. He was crying. *Crying!* I'd never seen Dad cry, and it scared me, hearing it now. Mom's footsteps echoed across the tiled floor.

There was a long, long pause and I could tell they were hugging.

"I haven't been brave, Dan. I buried things, important things, willed them to just *go away*. And I dragged you into it, too."

"It was my decision, Abbe," Dad said. "Whatever it is, I love you."

"I know," she sniffled. "I love you too. And M. So much. It's just . . . I need some time to figure out so much. . . ." Then—"Oh, Danno—," Mom started to cry, "I've done such a terrible job mothering."

The surprise of her words took my breath away. And listening there, on the stairs, I felt a new kind of scared and it wasn't because of the crying.

In the fading light, I roll down the steep embankment, passing a few people without saying hello. I've since decided that Dad moved us here because without Mom's salary at the hospital, it's cheap. Nothing more than a bunch of run-down floats hooked up to rotting pilings and bobbing on the tides. Peeling green paint and dying potted plants everywhere.

"Hey, sweetie," Dad greets me, squinting against the setting sun. "How goes it?"

He's sitting on the warped planks of the houseboat's outer deck, tying up some newspapers with twine. I step over the rope fence and try to slide quickly past, avoiding his worried eyes. But he gets up and follows me inside anyway, trailing behind like a pet. That just makes me even sadder, reminding me of another casualty of Mom's leaving, my lost cat, Blackberry.

"Hungry?"

I shake my head. "No, thanks," I lie. My backpack hits the floor with a thud. "I've got tons of homework." I start down the tiny hall and almost make it to my room.

"Did you stop at the PO on the way home?"

I shake my head no again and keep walking.

"O-kaaaaay," Dad says, stretching out the word. "Well, come on out later if you change your mind about dinner . . . or want to talk."

Without turning, I nod and push the door closed, wishing for the umpteenth time that I wasn't an only child. I throw myself down on my narrow bed, the houseboat swaying with the sudden movement, and stare up at the ceiling.

Talk. That's all Dad wants to do now, but it feels too late to talk.

Mom tried to talk too, that night before she left. She came into my room and switched on the light, but I was furious. I jumped out of bed and flicked it back off. I didn't want to look at her, or hear anything she had to say. So we had our last conversation in the dark. Only it wasn't a conversation really, it was more like a fight.

"It's complicated, M. I don't know how to explain it all right now," Mom said. "I'm sorry." She reached out to stroke my hair but I pulled away from her touch. "So dark . . . and wavy," she went on anyway. "Just like my mother's."

Silence. More waiting. Finally, Mom let out a sigh.

"I know what I'm asking is huge, M. But I need you to trust me. I can't do this alone. You're such a capable girl. Can you be strong for me now, Marisa?" She stopped and waited, but I was determined not to say a word. I had no clue what she was talking about or what it had to do with me.

Until I remembered what she'd said to Dad that night in the kitchen. The words shot through me like a bolt, scaring me all over again.

"I just need some time, M. I'll be back. But it's the only—"

"So GO!" I shouted. "I know you want to! Just go!" I flung my foot out and kicked. Mom jumped up. The hurt . . . the fear . . . I couldn't stand it anymore.

"No! Marisa, that's not what I'm say—"

"You don't care about *anything* anymore! Not Dad, or me or anything! So just go!"

"Honey, please. I need to—"

"Take all the time you want! I don't care if you EVER come back! GO!"

With that last scream, I scrunched down in bed, pulled the covers over my head, and didn't move again until after I heard the bedroom door close.

Long minutes passed. I waited there in the dark, my brain zipping back and forth between being so angry my body couldn't stop shaking and another part thinking I should jump up and run into the hall after her. I kept waiting for the door to open again, waiting for Mom to come back in, smooth my hair and tell me everything was going to be okay, she wasn't going anywhere, she was staying right there with me. I waited and waited, until I fell asleep waiting.

When I woke up, I could feel it—she was gone. An empty space opened up someplace deep inside me, filled with a fluttery fear that's stayed trapped inside ever since. For days, my mind raced, thinking surely she'd come back soon. But she didn't.

I've taken to counting the slats on the old houseboat ceiling, so I already know there are eighteen going from left to right, but now I count them again anyway. From the tiny window set at eye level to my bed, I can just see the edge of the Narrows as it curves up toward the open inlet and the tip of the Warren Avenue Bridge. I lay silent, trying to steady my breathing. Outside, the sky goes from deep purple to near black and the moon begins its slow rise.

Across the room, on my dresser, an envelope sits propped against the oval mirror. That next morning, when I woke up to find Mom had really gone, I also found that letter, written with one of Mom's favorite blue felt-tip pens. I read it at lightning speed in an angry blur of emotions, then shoved it back into its envelope.

Since that morning, I've reread that letter probably fifty times looking for some clue, some reason why she really left. I've got the whole darn thing memorized and could recite it out loud right now to you, down to her last two words.

But there's nothing in it that explains anything. I groan and sink back on my bed. I don't need any more letters from Mom that don't make any sense. One is enough.

———

M—

I knew this would be hard, but it's so much worse than I expected. I've rewritten this letter a dozen times and still it doesn't feel right. Writing words no one would want to read. They would sound every bit as wrong if I were saying them to you in person.

Something happened to me years ago, M. Something I never expected. I don't know how I've managed to avoid it all these years, but I can't avoid it any longer. Have you ever done that? Pretended something would just go away? It's so easy to do. I thought that with time, things would change. And they did, but not the way I'd planned.

I've been given a second chance, M, and I need to find the courage to take it.

Do you remember how we used to love to walk across the Warren Ave Bridge and look all up and down the inlet? How sometimes, it was only from that vantage point that we could tell which direction the salmon were running? Well, it's taken me 24 years and 1,140 miles to finally see which way I was running. I can't go back in time and change what happened, but I can make it right now. And I'm beginning to think that's the only way for me to move forward, by looking back.

I love you, Marisa. I'll write again, I promise. Trust me.

And I'm coming back. Trust me on that, too.

Be good, Mom

CHAPTER 3

Orca Day 2

M_arisa_. Honey...wake up."

Dad sits on the edge of my bed, lightly scratching my back, his special way of waking me since I was a little girl. The tiny window facing the bay is still dark.

"What time is it?" I ask, my voice groggy. Waking up still doesn't feel the same. A minute of calm, then a rush of remembering.

"Just six," Dad says. "Tal phoned. He wants me in early."

Tal Reese owns Mud Bay Kayak Center, where Dad's the manager. But before Mom left, Dad had his own carpentry projects too. Now it feels like he's always going in to Mud Bay early or staying late. I wonder sometimes if we both avoid each other for the same reasons.

I shiver and pull the covers closer around me. Sometimes living on this houseboat is like being _in_ the water instead of just on it. The ancient heater either delivers hot, dry air or it hardly works at all. In spite of everything, living here might actually be kind of fun except it only happened after Mom left.

"Listen," Dad continues as he rubs my back, "I have some good news."

I'm instantly awake, waiting to hear that Mom's back, sitting at our little kitchen counter, drinking a cup of tea. "A bunch of *whales* are swimming around in the inlet. Seems people have been calling and leaving messages since last night to reserve boats. That sure doesn't happen every day, huh?" Even without looking, I can tell Dad is smiling. I sink back into my pillow, disappointed, and try to think of what to say.

"Hey, I know it's a school day, but what do you think about coming along? Remember that camp you went to up in the San Juans a couple summers ago? You came home pretty psyched." Dad shifts on the bed and chuckles to himself. "Plastered your walls with pictures and those pod genealogies . . . all sorts of stuff."

The chilly morning and Dad's memory stir up the familiar tug of missing what I don't have anymore. I lie there quiet in my cold bed, and part of me wants so much to throw myself into Dad's arms and just cry. But then Dad will want to "talk." I haven't been in the mood to talk for a long time.

"I kidded you no end that you must have been a whale in a previous life—thick black hair, white skin, just like—" he stops, realizing where his talk has gotten him. "Anyway . . ." he coughs. "You up for it?" He starts rubbing my back again but I squirm out from underneath and roll onto my side to face the wall.

Has he forgotten who really loved whales? Who would have been crazy with excitement if she were here?

"Umm, I don't think so," I mutter into my pillow. "Today's our science unit exam," I lie.

"Well . . . this is kind of science in action."

After a long minute, Dad bends down and kisses the top of my head and I feel myself relax. I know he won't argue. Dad never argues, not even when Mom said she needed to leave. Not one fight.

I still can't believe how this all happened without any fights. Neither of us fought for Mom to stay.

I shift in my bed, restless. For a long time, feeling angry seemed safer than feeling anything else, but now mostly what I'm really feeling is confused.

I can still see them both standing there, holding hands, telling me everything will be okay. *Trust us,* they said. *Mom just needs some time.* For the hundredth time, I'm certain I must have missed something. Otherwise, it doesn't make any sense. Mom says she needs time to figure stuff out. Dad says sure, fine. And that's it? She leaves, we move to the marina, and everything in our lives changes?

Maybe they did all their fighting when I wasn't around. Or maybe it was something else totally, something too horrible to tell. Was Mom already married to somebody else when she met Dad? Is that why she's keeping the truth from him too, even now? Or is she running from the law? I barely know where she grew up—somewhere in California—she was always vague about it. And I never knew my grandparents, which is too bad, because if they were still alive, I'd call them up right now and get some answers.

But none of that feels really right. I keep coming back to the one thing that makes more sense than any of the others: Mom's leaving had something to do with me. Why else would she tell Dad she was a terrible mother?

"Eat something, okay?" Dad's voice startles me back to the present. "Maybe they'll still be here later." He stands up. "And . . ." he pauses dramatically, "I'm going to trust you to ride by the PO after school, okay?"

The question hangs in the air. And this time Dad won't leave until he gets a nod from me. When he opens the front door to go, a gust of even colder air blows in. As he steps outside, the houseboat pitches and sways, then slowly settles back, rocking me in my bed. I lie there in the dark, remembering that summer two years ago. Mom was so excited when she found the whale camp—she'd checked out everything offered within a fifty-mile radius of Seattle looking for the "perfect experience." It was where I first met Lena. We spent three weeks kayaking and studying marine biology—and becoming best buds. It all seems like centuries ago now.

Getting up quickly, I skitter across the narrow hallway into the kitchen and prop open the door to help the struggling heater push warmer air toward my bed. Then I climb back under the covers, stretching out my legs. My toes are freezing and I miss Blackberry again. He used to sleep on my feet, kept them nice and toasty.

But he ran away, too. Just like Mom. I try hard to push away all my gloomy thoughts, but I have as much luck as the houseboat heater.

———

Downtown Manette is really just a couple of blocks of small family-owned businesses, most of them having something to do with camping or fishing. Places with names like "Sugar Shack" and "Trail's End." Evanston Memorial is here too, the hospital where Mom worked. Sometimes, we'd meet after school if she could arrange her shift, and walk a couple of blocks over to the town pool to swim or use the "spa"—just a hot tub really. Besides collecting the mail, those memories are another good reason to avoid coming here now.

Picking up our mail from the Manette PO box has been my job since I've been old enough to bike here alone. Charlie Taffett, the postmaster, used to keep an eye on me when I was littler. If it wasn't busy, sometimes he'd let me help him attach labels to packages or practice my numbers by reading the weight off the scale. I loved it. Now my goal is get in and out without any collateral damage. Even worse, now the trips have the added pressure of reporting back to Dad.

The post office is nearly empty. I sneak in as quietly as I can, trying to avoid Charlie's notice, which isn't that hard really, because Charlie is pretty old, and always seems to be pulling off his glasses for some reason. I dig out my key, open our box, and pull out a thick bundle. It's the usual mix of junk mail, bills, and a few magazines, some still addressed to Mom, and I suddenly decide to let Dad deal with it all at home. Then, just as I'm shoving the whole stack into my backpack, I catch sight of it—a slim white envelope with blue felt-tip pen writing.

I check the postmark—"PASADENA, CA."

So, she did go home. And the thought that *my* home isn't Mom's anymore makes my stomach queasy. I take one more second to feel the letter's thickness, silently calculating how many sheets of paper might be inside. Then, after a quick glance around, as if I'm doing something illegal, I slip the letter into the narrow slot of the blue plastic recycling bin.

The minute it drops down, I feel a pang of regret. But the post office feels like it's suddenly crowded with people—I can't very well take the lid off and fish it back out. At least that's what I tell myself. Besides, it's probably just more words that don't make sense anyway. Not the real truth.

———

Mud Bay Kayak and Rowing Center sits tucked into a small bay on the southwest side of the inlet, across the bridge and a bike ride away from Olympic Junior High.

"Hey!" Dad sees me and calls out, taking a break from wetting down the dock. "I've been waiting for you."

I glide down the Veneta Street hill. It's a weekday but the dock is crowded, with more people out in boats than on an ordinary weekend. "Has it been like this all day?"

Dad's boss, Tal, overhears my question and walks over to join us. "This is the slowest it's been!" he laughs.

I like Tal. He's a big man with a bushy beard and wrinkled skin from too many days spent outdoors. I usually only see him when I visit Dad at Mud Bay, but he always seems so relaxed, like he doesn't have a care in the world. Not like Dad . . . or me.

Plus he's always full of weird facts and trivia, mostly history and science stuff.

"In fact," he turns to me, "I'd say the crowds have been rather *fervid*, or if you prefer, *perfervid*. Interestingly, the two words mean the same thing," Tal says. "Just like *flammable* and *inflammable*."

Tal and I have this game where he quizzes me by using tricky words that hardly anybody knows and I have to figure out what they mean. Once he found out I was interested in science, the words got harder. I don't always get them right, but I usually look them up later. It's actually kind of fun.

"Marisa? What's your guess?"

"Umm, *enthusiastic*?" Tal waits. He wants more specifics. "*Feverish*?"

"Good girl! Comes from the Latin *fervere*, 'to boil.'" He pats me on the shoulder. "It's unbelievable, actually," he adds, shaking his head. "Be interesting to see how long they stay—"

"Wait," I interrupt, "the people or the whales? Have they been out there this whole time?"

"Seems so," Dad says. "We haven't seen them." He runs his hands through his brown curls, giving his head a scratch. "But apparently they're feeding big-time."

"Is that why they're here, you think?"

"I don't think anybody really knows," Tal answers. "Could be they followed in a wave of the chum. Chico Creek's one of the last good runs around. Well, I'd better start closing down shop or we'll never get out of here. Bright and early tomorrow, Dan!" he calls back as he heads inside.

I stare out over the inlet. Already, the sky is darkening. Once the sun dips down behind the mountains, the light here goes fast. Dad turns off the water and tosses down the hose. He follows my gaze, then sits down on the grass beside me.

"Any mail?"

I hand over the bundle of magazines and bills, but shake my head no. I know what Dad really means, and for a split second, I feel a rush of guilt but quickly push it away.

Dad takes the mail, but stares at me.

"Marisa, I know what you did."

I freeze, thinking he somehow knows about the recycled letter, but he couldn't.

"Lena stopped by. She told me you guys saw the whales yesterday when you were out fishing." Dad's lips are pressed together in a pout. His eyes get that hurt puppy-dog expression. "Why didn't you say anything to me this morning?"

I turn away quickly, and stare at the wooden slats of the dock. Why won't you tell *me* the real reason Mom left?

I shrug. "It didn't seem like a big deal."

"You see the orcas up close in the inlet and you don't think that's a big enough deal to tell me?" Dad sighs a big sigh. I pick at the long grass, ripping out small bits and rolling them into little balls with my fingers. "If you won't talk to me about a whale sighting . . . something that you care so much about—"

"I just didn't, okay?" I cut him off, aiming the grass pellets out toward the dock in perfect trajectories. When they hit, they relax and lose their tightly wound shape.

"No, Marisa, it's not okay." He stands and starts to pace back and forth in front of me. "Look, you know I'm not one to pressure, but a good attitude goes a long way."

This is so far from what I was expecting to hear that I sit there, speechless.

"I know you're struggling—but we have to work together," Dad says. "I don't know all the answers about why Mom left, and I'm not happy about it either. But I trust her. And you should too. Things aren't as hopeless as you're making them out to be." He pauses, waiting. "C'mon," he whispers. "Where's my best girl? I miss her."

I jump to my feet, the sudden movement shifting something inside me. The wooden dock in front of me is littered now with green flecks.

"I don't *know* where she is, Dad. Maybe she's gone!" My words come spitting out, sarcastic and cruel, hitting him as I turn and walk away. "Maybe she left with Mom."

CHAPTER 4

Orca Day 3

Okay, everybody, listen up."

Third period, just before lunch, our science teacher Mr. O'Connor works to keep the class settled for another twenty minutes.

"*Orcinus orca.*" He writes on the blackboard as the room quiets. "The scientific name for killer whales. Phylum of Chordata, Class Mammalia." More writing. "Order Cetacea. Suborder Odontoceti, and the Family . . . is Delphinidae."

He pauses to let his writing catch up to his voice. Except for me, everyone is busy writing the classification order in their notebooks.

"Killer whales are the largest members of Delphinidae, a group that also includes porpoises and dolphins. And they remain the TOP predators in the ocean." He underlines "TOP" three times. "They have only one enemy . . . humans."

A low murmur runs through the room.

"Remember people, just like dolphins and porpoises, whales live in the ocean, but they are not fish! They're mammals, and like all mammals they have lungs not gills. And what do we do with our lungs?" Mr. O'Connor raises his hands like a conductor. "C'mon, all together now—"

"Breathe!" a few scattered voices call out.

"Breathe *what?*"

"BREATHE AIR!" everyone shouts together.

"Okay, good. Now, the last reported sighting of orcas in Dyes Inlet was about forty years ago, in the late 1950s. I was just a wee tyke then, toddling along," he adds in a silly voice. The class laughs. Everybody likes Mr. O'Connor. He's funny and loud and somehow manages to jam two years' worth of work into 7/8 Science. If you keep up, there's a good chance you can test out of freshman bio in high school.

"So IF the average life expectancy of killer whales in the wild is thirty to fifty years, AND only a few out there are thirty-five or older...." He gestures to the windows that face out toward the inlet, "... what can we infer about our nineteen visitors?"

The class is quiet. Fifteen seconds. Mr. O'Connor coughs. Thirty.

"C'mon! Who's our math whiz?"

"Maybe ..." Lena offers, "some of them have never been here before?"

"Precisely!" Mr. O'Connor jabs at the air like a marathon winner, the chalk still in his hand. "Everybody put your fins together for Lena!" The class claps halfheartedly, some kids rolling their eyes at Mr. O'Connor. I glance over at Lena and she gives me a thumbs-up.

"These are very likely unknown waters to the majority of these whales. So as long as they remain—and how long that will be is anyone's guess—we have an extraordinary opportunity to learn about them. Kind of like having a new kid move across the bridge."

He means the Warren Avenue Bridge, the main link that connects the east and west sections of Port Washington. Around here everything depends on which side of the bridge you live on—how much money you have, who your friends are, what you'll do when you grow up. There's only one thing we all share—Dyes Inlet.

"Now," Mr. O'Connor spins around to face the class, "who can tell me what the basic social unit of whales is called?"

"A school!" someone calls out.

Mr. O'Connor smiles but shakes his head.

"A herd?"

It's Harris, a hard-to-ignore kid from one of the trailer parks on the west side of the bridge. The class laughs. He catches my eye and grins but I look away. Harris has the thickest black hair I've ever seen, besides mine. He's so tall he has to twist his legs every which way to get them to fit in under the desks. And he's *old*—almost fourteen.

"Herd is close, but no cigar," Mr. O'Connor says, flicking an imaginary cigar in front of his mouth.

More animal groups are called out. Then it gets too silly and Mr. O'Connor starts to lose patience. Why isn't anybody answering? I drum my fingers on my desk. I can't be the only one who knows this.

"Do any of you actually *live here* in the Pacific Northwest?" He waits, tapping his chalk on the desk. "Please! Someone?"

Finally I raise my hand. Mr. O'Connor points his invisible cigar at me.

"A pod."

"A *pod*. Thank you, Marisa." He stretches out his hand to me and makes a small bow. "Orca groups are called pods. They're extremely complex social structures. One pod can comprise the extended family unit of as many as four generations traveling together." He gestures toward the inlet again. "Our visitors here are part of the Southern Resident killer whales in the San Juan Islands that have three pods: J, K, and L."

At the mention of L Pod, a jumble of memories flashes through my mind, and the room feels suddenly as hot as a summer day.

"What's with the letters, Mr. O?" Harris calls out. A few people snicker.

"Actually, it's a good question," Mr. O'Connor replies. "It's a taxonomic system developed by whale researchers up in British Columbia. They started with 'A' and worked their way through the alphabet as they studied the pods to the south."

"Cool!" Harris says. "Kinda like Triple-A baseball."

"Each whale is given an alphanumeric code. The letter represents the pod affiliation, and the number is each individual identified within that pod. The smallest social unit within a pod is the 'matrilineal group.' Can someone please enlighten us as to the meaning of *matrilineal*?"

I'm only half listening, remembering instead a super hot Fourth of July that Mom and I spent up on San Juan Island . . . it seems so long ago now. I was probably eight years old and every memory I have from that trip is perfect. Dad was working a month-long carpentry job on the west side of the island and staying on the jobsite, so Mom and I came up for a week to visit.

The house was on an amazing bluff that overlooked the main straits where the Southern Resident orcas travel in the summer months. Every day we'd see the whales passing back and forth—breaching, jumping, and chasing each other in circles. Some days we'd climb down the rocky slope past the old abandoned limekiln to Deadman Bay. From the beach there, the orcas' huge fins looked even more gigantic. One morning, I was poking around in the sand looking for agates when Mom called to me from farther down the beach.

"M! Come look . . . I think the pod has a new baby!"

I scrambled over to where she stood on the rocks peering out at the water, Dad's old black binoculars glued to her eyes. "Where?" I asked, already reaching out to have a look.

"There." She passed me the binoculars and pointed. "See? Just past the big one . . . he's tucked in close to his mother."

I looked and looked until finally I saw a little black head poke up alongside the shiny black flank of the mother whale. But the little orca was black and *orange*, not black and white like the others! I thought the sun might be playing tricks on me.

"Why is he that funny color?" I asked. "Is he okay?"

"Yes, he's fine," Mom said, snapping some pictures with her camera. "Isn't that amazing? Nobody knows why the calves start out that color. The orange will fade to white as he grows. Wouldn't it be funny if human babies were born orange?"

We both laughed, sitting together on the hot rocks, watching the baby orca nuzzle its mother. The next day, Mom and I went down to the Whale Museum in Friday Harbor, the island's main town, to report that we'd sighted a new orca baby.

"Yours is the first sighting of a new calf this season!" the woman in the museum told us. She checked her logs. "It looks like that was L Pod out near Lime Kiln yesterday. The official name will be L91 but would you like to pick a nickname for him?" she asked, smiling.

"Would you, honey?" Mom repeated, putting her arm around my shoulder.

I took a bite of raw carrot and thought about what to name the new baby orca.

"Muncher!" I announced a minute later. Mom laughed and the museum woman carefully wrote out an adoption certificate for Muncher.

"Congratulations," she said, handing me the sheet of paper. "Now you be sure to take good care of Muncher."

"I will," I promised. "Muncher can be my baby brother!"

"Well, we don't know yet if he's a boy or girl," the museum woman said with a laugh.

A lost memory comes rushing back to me now: Mom's reaction was . . . odd. She looked surprised and then something else, sort of sad, I guess. I remember asking her what was wrong, but she didn't answer. Just shook her head and smiled. I'd forgotten that even happened until now.

The sound of paper and shuffling feet snaps me back to the present. I look up and Mr. O'Connor is staring right at me.

"Umm . . . sorry, what was the question?" I quickly try to catch up.

"Matrilineal group. What does that mean for orcas?"

The whole class sits waiting for me to answer. Mr. O'Connor tilts his head. He *knows* I know, but I can't answer this one. I shake my head no, concentrating on my sneakers instead.

"All right then," he says, annoyed at having to answer his own question. "Matrilineal groups are pods made up of two or three generations that share a close female ancestor, usually a mother and grandmother. Offspring travel and stay with their mother and her pod for life."

My heart hurts. Hands down orcas are better at parenting than some humans. *My* humans, for example.

"Now . . . our visitors number nineteen animals, mostly females and their calves, with a handful of frisky adolescent males."

I check the clock. Five more minutes.

"A team of experts are on their way down from Friday Harbor. Marine biologists and whale researchers. *Cetologists*—note that the word derives from the order name."

Chairs scrape. A few people cough.

"They've asked me to round up some volunteers. Mostly the work will be hauling equipment around, helping set up traffic barriers, grunt work for the grunts." Mr. O'Connor smiles and passes around a sign-up sheet. "But they've promised to include educational opportunities when they can, depending on how long the whales stay, of course. . . ." The bell rings and a few kids start to stand up, but Mr. O'Connor isn't finished. "Wait . . . you'll also earn community service hours and get firsthand exposure to science in action!"

There's a flurry of activity as everyone gathers their stuff and scrambles for the door.

"Extra credit!" Mr. O'Connor shouts.

I can't seem to move. Mom kept trying to plan our whale-watching trip for this summer, I kept saying no. Is this *my* second chance? I steal a glance at Lena. She's already at the front of the sign-up line, her mind made up. She sees me look and waves me over. My head is pounding. I stand up and leave the room fast, before Lena can stop me.

Maybe that trip with Mom would have made a difference, but now it feels too late. And all the community services hours in the world aren't going to bring Mom back.

CHAPTER 5

The lunchroom is buzzing with everyone chattering about Mr. O'Connor's extra credit project. Listening to some conversations, you'd think he'd promised they'd get to swim underwater with the whales instead of hauling trash and directing traffic. I try to slip in and out unnoticed, but no luck. Harris sees me and waves me over. Somehow, Lena is already magically there, along with Grace, a thin, pale girl with deep blue eyes. I sit down at their table and Grace looks at me with the same expression she always gives me: *Oh, you again.*

"Why *not* do it?" Harris is saying. "We get excused from all afternoon classes if we sign up. Besides, I got some free time now that my old man's showed up again."

"Because it's going to be work," Lena reminds him. "Not just time off school."

Harris sips his pop and shrugs. "How hard can it be?"

"Harder than most stuff *you've* ever done," Grace says, her voice flat.

Lena shoots her a look, but Harris just grins.

"You don't know hard," he laughs, looking Grace in the eye. Then he turns to me. "You sign up, Marisa?"

I feel my face redden. A simple "no" won't do it, because it's sure to be followed by "why?" And that's complicated, just like Harris's life, or at least that's what I used to think before *my* life got complicated. It's no secret that Harris is in charge of his little brother, Jesse, when their dad's not around, which seems to be most of the time. I wouldn't even know Harris or Jesse at all if it weren't for Mom's volunteering at the youth shelter. Mom again.

I fumble to open my lunch and decide to ignore his question when Lena smoothly answers for me instead.

"Heck yes, we're going."

I stare at her. "What are you talking about? I didn't sign up...."

"I know. I signed us both up." She smiles, eating a handful of grapes. "What are friends for?"

"You can't *do* that," I whisper. "You can't just go signing other people's names for things!" Grace snickers and I lower my voice, "Besides... *I can't do it.*"

"Why not?"

"I . . . I'm too busy," I stammer. "I can't miss all those afternoon classes."

"Right," Lena says, frowning. "Gotta make sure you bring your 'A' in Language Arts up to 'A+'. What happened to your famous Love of Science?"

"That's not the point!" I jump up. "You can't just go making decisions for other people!" I feel my face starting to flush. Everybody's listening. Grace sticks out her lower lip, giving me a fake "poor you" look.

How can I explain? I can't shake the weird feeling that I'm just moving through days, going through the motions, when really I should be doing something more important, like trying to find Mom and bring her home.

"Well, it's too late," Lena says simply. "Oh come on, Marisa, when else will you have a chance like this?" She crumples up her lunch bag and looks at me hard. "Ever since fifth grade you've been going on and on about how awesome orcas are, you've dragged me to whale movies, you play whale songs on your Walkman...."

I sigh, listening. There's nothing to say without outright lying. She's right.

"You even did one of those whale adoption things with your mom, didn't you?"

I stop her right there.

"Look . . . I told you, I'm *not* going." My voice sounds louder and meaner than I intended.

She frowns and leads me away from the others. "Listen, Marisa. I'm not stupid. I know things are weird for you since your mom left." I cringe, but she doesn't back off. "But you won't talk to me about it. So I have to do *something.*"

I start to protest but she holds up her palm.

"You owe it to me to at least *try.*" She spins in place and is gone before I can even open my mouth to say "no" again.

——

It's almost six-thirty by the time I get home. I glide down the marina embankment and heave my bike over the wharf's edge, securing it against the leeward wall. When I unlock the front door, it's dark inside—Dad's not home yet. I turn on the light and slump down on the couch, not moving until my growling stomach gets my attention. No homemade dinner waiting for you, Marisa. Looking around the quiet room, it's so easy to feel sorry for myself again.

Irritated, I punch the TV button on and head to the kitchen, hoping I can find something fast and easy to eat. I open the door and the refrigerator whirs to life, but what's inside is pretty bleak. Not much more than an almost empty jar of peanut butter, yellowing broccoli, and some questionable egg salad.

Not like before. Dad and I used to cook together, a lot. Lemon chicken. Six-onion soup. A spicy red pasta sauce made with garlic, capers, olives, and anchovies that Dad said was named for the "Italian Ladies of the Night." We always made it on special occasions because it was the dish Dad was cooking when he first met Mom years ago. The story goes that she was waitressing at a Pioneer Square steakhouse and putting herself through nursing school in Seattle. Dad had taken a job as a fry cook. Mom said one of the things she loved about him was how he would sear steaks wearing a tie that he'd throw over his shoulder. "I took one look and knew he'd be a special guy," she laughed.

Mom was never big on birthday parties but each year, she'd let Dad dress up with a white shirt and tie, toss it over his shoulder, and cook her up a big batch of *Pasta Puttanesca* for her birthday. As I got older, he let me help. But this year was different. Mom sat at the table, staring out the big window that faced west toward the inlet. It was like she wanted to be anywhere else but here with us.

"Happy Birthday, Abbe," Dad had said, coming up from behind and ceremoniously laying a plate of pasta down in front of her. Then he kissed her on her neck. "I love you," I heard him whisper.

Mom's eyes flickered and she looked as if she was going to burst into tears. She didn't, but she didn't smile either. She didn't do anything. We ate our dinner in almost complete silence.

"C'mon, Abbe, you know how I love cooking this for your birthday," Dad said, after awhile, "Don't disappoint us—"

"It's easy to disappoint, isn't it?" Mom said. "We try and try and still we let so many people down. . . ."

She wasn't really talking to us. I tried to catch her eye but it was like she didn't even know I was there.

"I thought I was being brave. All these years. . . ."

"Abbe, honey—" Dad pleaded.

"Stop," Mom turned and looked at him sharply. "This is wrong. It's just *all wrong*."

And with that, Mom stood up. I can still hear the sound of her chair scraping on the wood floor as she pushed it roughly back. A minute later, I heard the door slam as she left the house.

I remember turning to Dad, not understanding. Wrong about what? I asked, but he didn't answer. Didn't or wouldn't. But I'd never seen him look so sad.

The sound of tinny music on the TV wheedles way into my head. The evening news is starting its wrap-up.

"And that's it for tonight, folks. But before we sign off, Stacy, can you give us an update on our marine visitors?"

"I sure can, Jake. We now know that the whales in Dyes Inlet belong to a subgroup of orcas that summer here in Puget Sound known as L Pod. Researchers are worried that they might be lost, Jake, because these are unknown waters for these whales."

"And I understand they've identified nineteen whales?"

"That's right, Jake. L Pod is really one big happy family. Each whale has a name as well as an assigned number: Faith, Canuck, Muncher—"

I stand there, frozen, the refrigerator door open. Did I hear that right?

"They're going to be monitoring them closely to be sure they're not showing any signs of stress."

"Well, Stacy, they look pretty relaxed to me."

Jake and Stacy continue to banter with each other, laughing at their own jokes. I slam the refrigerator door shut so hard it shudders, then click off the TV. It's suddenly and pleasantly quiet again.

I try to think back if I ever learned how whales behave when they're stressed, but I can't remember. I'm pretty sure Jake and Stacy don't know. Do they get quiet and forget to eat? Do they leave the pod and swim off by themselves?

Back in my room, I push aside a pile of papers and notebooks lying in front of the chest, and pull open the bottom drawer. It's packed tight. There was so much stuff that I had to throw out when we moved from East Sixteenth Street that I'm not sure what's left and what got tossed, but I start looking anyway. I riffle through half-used sheets of wrapping paper, folded-up posters, paintings and watercolors from art classes. I recognize a couple of drawings that I made for Mother's Day cards. My throat catches a little and I push them aside.

Finally, I see what I'm looking for. Carefully, I pull it out and lay it on the bed, flattening it as well as I can on the soft surface. The title, running across the full width of the sheet, in black italic caps, stares up at me:

L POD ADOPTION CERTIFICATE: L91 "MUNCHER"

I sit back on my knees and breathe deeply.

Four-year-old Muncher—the little whale Mom and I adopted —was back.

CHAPTER 6

Orca Day 4

Saturday morning traffic is bumper-to-bumper on Tracyton Boulevard, the narrow winding road that hugs the inlet shoreline. Dad drums his fingers on the steering wheel. Slumped in the front seat, I fidget.

"Just drop me off here," I say. "I'll walk the rest of the way." I know if I wait much longer, I'll be tempted to tell him to turn around and go home.

"You sure you're okay?"

"I'm fine." I wish he would stop asking me that, because the lie always feels like it's pushing him further away.

"Let me know if I can do anything, okay?"

I reach behind to grab my backpack from the backseat, open the door, and step out. Should I ask him to do a U-turn and start driving south to California?

"I'll call later," I say, slamming the door before Dad can ask anything else.

After the stuffiness of the car, the cool air coming off the inlet is a relief. It's weird seeing my usually sleepy town like this, full of people—strangers. At every side street, more cars are heading down to the water. Maybe before, it would be exciting. Right now, it just makes me feel lonely.

"Just in time," Lena says, running to meet me. "I thought maybe you would chicken out." I shrug, deciding it's better not to say anything, and follow behind as we head down to the water.

The Tracyton boat launch is really just a poured slab of concrete, maybe twenty feet wide, added to the end of the road and angled down so that a boat can enter the water. Today, it's jam-packed with people: some like us who are here to volunteer, but others who just seem curious. I take a steadying breath and survey all the activity.

"Who's that with Mr. O?"

Lena shrugs. "Some whale guy from Friday Harbor."

The whale guy is tall, with broad shoulders and wild, rumpled hair. He kind of reminds me of Dad. Next to him, Mr. O'Connor looks even thinner and paler than he usually does under our classroom's fluorescent lights. Both of them are outfitted for a big expedition, with clipboards, radios, and beepers hooked to their belts. All sorts of stuff lies scattered at their feet—a pile of life jackets, caps, water bottles, cameras. I peer down into an open box. More binoculars.

"What exactly are we going to be doing?" I ask Lena nervously. "I thought it was just grunt work."

Lena shakes her head. "Not sure. I just got here." She takes my arm and nudges us closer to the front of the group where outdoors guy is opening up a marine chart. Two kids hold it up so we can all see—a map of Dyes Inlet. "Hey, whatever it is, we'll stick together. C'mon—"

"This is day four, and the start of a weekend," the whale guy explains. I can tell from his accent that he's not from around here.

Maybe somewhere in the South? "I'm sure y'all have noticed the whales' visit has attracted just a *few* people." Laughter ripples through the crowd.

"These guys have a habit of sticking their noses into inlets all over the place." He traces around the outline of the inlet with his pencil. "Dyes Inlet opens up like a balloon once you're through the Narrows and past Rocky Point, but it's still pretty confined. It's a little too early to be alarmed, but better safe than sorry. These are big animals. They need room. We're going to want to keep people off the water and encourage them to watch from shore instead. We're coordinating with the National Marine Fisheries Service to help with that."

"Volunteers, we need your help," Mr. O'Connor looks at us. "To load and unload the rafts, to set up barriers, to walk the shoreline and pass out whale watching guidelines, to man the info table, and generally to answer visitor questions with proficiency and aplomb, as the *Orcinus orca* experts I know you all are." He pauses then grins at us. "And for those of you who are seaworthy, we'll need help on the water too, especially tomorrow when we place the hydrophones that let us 'listen' to the whales."

I fidget and glance at Lena who's listening closely. I should do it now. Tell her I can't stay long.

"Don't worry," the whale guy adds. "We'll work closely with y'all, give you some training. But I've got a sneaky suspicion these big guys are gonna draw some crowds, so we'll need all the helping hands we can get. Any questions?"

"Who *are* you?" Lena calls out. The crowd of volunteers turns toward us, laughing, and my chance to duck out disappears. "Sorry, I was stuck in traffic," she adds, smiling.

"Not a problem. I'm Kevin Brooks, from the Center for Whale Research in Friday Harbor. My primary work with whales is behavioral—I study why they act the way they do. I'm also the 'fin-guy'!" He sets his hand on his head and wiggles his fingers.

Everyone is quiet, wondering what in the world he's doing.

"I can pretty much recognize any North Pacific orca at a glance, just by their dorsal fins," he explains, "which I'm pretty proud of, if I do say so myself."

"Cool!" a familiar voice calls out. I turn and spot Harris a few heads back, standing with his little brother, Jesse.

"Lastly, I also direct SoundKeeper," Kevin continues. "That's the volunteer program y'all will be helping with. Whale watching is a great opportunity to learn about marine mammals and Sound-Keeper's mission is to teach folks how to do it right."

"What's with the *y'all*?" Lena whispers but I shrug, distracted. "C'mon," she says, "let's sign up for water duty." And she's off like a shot to the front, not waiting for my answer. I watch her go, annoyed with myself again, when I feel something tug on my backpack.

Jesse. His tiny face stares up at me, smiling.

"Hell-lo Reeeesa. Reesa. Reesa!" he says in a singsong voice. He stretches his arms out for a hug.

"Hi. Where's Harris?" I ask, bending down and wrapping my arms around him.

He points toward the shoreline edge. "Off!"

"Did he leave you here alone?" I swivel around to look for Harris. Jesse just keeps smiling.

Jesse is different. He doesn't talk the way you'd expect from an eight-year-old. Mom knew his story. She used to talk to Dad about all the kids she worked with, trying to get them the help they needed. I try to remember exactly what she said about Jesse but can't. Was I even listening? Thinking about it bothers me now.

"Let's go find him and say hi, okay?"

Jesse smiles and nods. I take his hand and we move toward the boat launch. Jesse walks with a crooked sort of limp, the tips of his feet pointed outward. I spot Harris up ahead and quicken my pace, pulling Jesse along.

Near the dock, Harris is bent over, pawing through the pile of bright orange life jackets on the ground, looking for one that will fit. He's not having much luck.

"They musta thought we were all gonna be little kids," he jokes as Jesse runs up and parks himself on the ground between us. Harris finally settles on one that just about makes it around his chest.

He grins at me, proud, waving a sheet of paper in my face. "We're on the same team!"

"What!?" I take a step back.

"Mr. O put me on the boat with you and Lena. He says you're the best teacher around!"

"We're going out on the water . . . together?"

"You bet. No way I'm gonna miss this."

"Do you know anything about boats?"

"Nope," Harris shrugs. "Doesn't matter. Tons of people are going." Then he laughs. "You're going."

I watch him work at the life jacket buckles for a few seconds, then move closer so no one can overhear us. "What about Jesse?"

"What about him?"

"Who's going to watch him?"

"Jesse's cool. I take him lots of places. He can come with us."

Harris is treating this like it's no big deal, and it bothers me. How can he act as if everything is so—normal? Mom pops into my head again. I know what she would say. She'd tell Harris to go for it, and she'd help him out if he made mistakes.

But who cares what Mom thinks? She's not here.

"They want kids who know what they're doing," I blurt out. "What are you going to do if Jesse gets seasick?"

Harris freezes and stares at me.

"What're you trying to say?"

"Nothing . . . I . . . I just . . ." I stammer, realizing how mean I must sound. "It's just that you don't want to wind up being—"

"Being what?"

I hesitate, just a second too long.

"Being a *bother*?" he says.

Harris takes a step back. He rips off his life jacket and throws it on the dock, then turns away from me. I feel the blood rush to my face.

"Forget it," he growls, pulling Jesse to his feet. "Wouldn't want to be a *bother* to anyone, would we, Jes?" Jesse looks back and forth between us with wide black eyes.

"Harris, no . . . I just thought maybe you could help somewhere else—"

"You don't think I can do it," he spits out, spinning back to face me.

"No! It's not that—"

"Yeah, it is." He looks at me hard. "I thought you were different, Marisa. I thought you were like your mom."

I freeze, stunned to hear him bring up Mom.

"What's *that* supposed to mean? What does my mother have to do with this?"

"She *got* it," Harris says, not missing a beat. "But you don't, do you?"

I have no idea what he's talking about. "Got *what*?" I ask, already afraid of what he might answer.

Harris stares at me, like I should know.

"How it feels to be trapped. Folks look at you, get all twitchy.

They can only see one thing—tomorrow's loser." Jesse twirls around Harris, still holding on to his hand. "At first, I thought I was imagining it or going crazy. But she said no, what I was feeling was real. People judge me before they even know me." He gives me a long look. "She *got* it." Then he storms off the dock, dragging Jesse behind him. I stand there shaking, his words ringing in my ears.

All around me, people are getting ready to board the research float. It seems like only a minute has passed since I arrived at the dock and it seems like a day. Is Harris right? Was that what I was really thinking?

The first time I met Harris, I was probably ten years old, which would have made him about twelve, my age now. Mom had taken me with her to the youth shelter where she volunteered. Mostly she kept her daytime work separate from family. But she'd talk to me and Dad about the kids she worked with at the shelter, helping them with reading and schoolwork, things like that. Once a month she spent the night, supervising any kids who were staying overnight. Kids who got kicked out of their houses or some, like Harris and Jesse, who might need a night away once in a while from a parent on a drinking binge.

It would always be written on our kitchen calendar—the night Mom would be staying at the shelter. She'd lug her sleeping bag and a book to the car, and the next morning when I woke up she'd be back home. I remember always feeling it was as if she'd never really been gone.

I can't remember why I needed to go with Mom that night—maybe Dad was away on a carpentry job—but what I'll never forget is the feeling of wanting to be someplace else, anyplace but there at that shelter with those kids who were all so . . . *different*.

I walked behind Mom down the steps—the center was in the basement of a church hall. Through the grimy windows I could see a bunch of women and kids spreading out their sleeping bags and milling around. I stopped on the steps and wouldn't go any further. Mom reached out her hand to me but I wouldn't take it.

"What's wrong, sweetie?"

"I don't want to go in there," I whined. I stood there and wouldn't budge.

"Why? It'll be all right. I'll be with you." She peered in through windows that were at waist level. "Harris is here tonight! Remember I told you about him? He's a real character . . . you'll like him."

"I don't want to," I repeated, louder, meaner.

"Can you tell me why?" she asked, still patient.

I desperately wanted to turn and run away. Why didn't she understand? From inside the room I heard loud laughter and shivered.

"I'm afraid," I finally whispered.

Mom took a few steps back up the stairs and crouched down so that we were at eye level.

"Marisa," she said, "you don't have to be afraid. The people in there are just ordinary people, like you and me. They just haven't had the best of luck, maybe they made some bad choices. We all do. Now they just need a little extra help and somebody to believe in them is all." She paused to let her words sink in. "It's okay to need help, M. What's *not* okay is being too afraid to ask for it, or to reject somebody because of it."

I had no choice. She put her arm around me and together we walked down the steps to spend the night. More than two years later, I'm still standing on those steps, except Mom isn't here to help. Now all the choices are mine.

Harris and Jesse are already halfway back up the hill, Jesse running fast to keep up. At the top of the street, he turns around for one last look.

"Bye, Reeesa!" he yells down when he sees me watching, and smiles his big, innocent smile.

I sink down onto the grass, feeling like I might cry. Whatever energy I started out with this morning is completely gone now.

I messed up again, didn't I? First Mom, then Dad. Now Harris.

I'm not even sure I know what I'm fighting for anymore.

CHAPTER 7

Marisa? What's wrong?" Lena is suddenly at my side.

"Not now. . . ." Sitting on the cold ground, I try to stop my body from shaking. My eyes sting and my chest feels like it will burst. "Just leave me alone."

"No," Lena whispers. "I've told you a million times. I *won't* leave you alone." She looks around. "Where's Harris?"

Harris is gone, and he's right. Mom believed his story. It's me who doesn't believe it—his story or hers. *Me.*

"It doesn't matter," I shake my head, "you wouldn't understand."

"Try me," I hear Lena say. She pauses. "This is about your mom, isn't it? Tell me what happened."

I shake my head again, but she plops down beside me and waits. This time I know she won't let me off the hook.

"She left," I finally say. I can't look at her, but at least I've answered.

"Well, duh, I know *that*. I'm asking why. C'mon . . . you'll feel better if you talk about it."

"She just left. I don't know why."

"Marisa..." Lena sighs, exasperated. "There has to be more to the story than 'she just left.' What did she *say*?"

I shrug and look away, across the bright expanse of the inlet stretching out in front of us, suddenly wondering where Muncher is right now.

"You didn't *ask* her?" Lena guesses.

"It... it all happened so fast. One day she was there and then the next she was gone. I mean, I guess she tried to tell me... she wanted to talk the night before she left. And she sent me some letters...."

"And?" Lena stares at me with wide eyes.

I pause, not understanding.

"Her letters—what did she say in them?"

"I don't know, " I whisper. "I never read them."

"Well, hello!" Lena practically shouts. "That might be a good place to *start*."

I ignore her, hugging my knees closer to my chest.

She lets out a long breath. "Okay . . . what about your dad? What did he tell you?"

"He wants me to trust her," I shrug. "We haven't really talked much more about it...." There's a long pause as Lena takes in all this new information. It's the first time I've really told her anything. Suddenly, she jumps to her feet.

"I don't get it! I don't get you!" she says, raising her voice in frustration. "How can you not *talk* about where your mom is? My mother grills my dad when he goes *camping* for a weekend! Do you even know if she's coming back?"

"Well, that's the big question, isn't it?" I yell back at her, mad now for letting her drag me into talking. "Forget it. I *told you* you wouldn't understand." I glance over at the launch. "Just go already. They're getting ready to leave." I jump up and walk away quickly.

"Marisa!"

But I'm already gone.

———

I stumble along the shoreline trying to calm down. It doesn't work. All I want is for my life to be back the way it was—simple, ordinary, *normal*. What's so wrong with that? A wave of tiredness washes over me. The inlet and the beach look raw and dangerous, not inviting at all. I sink down on the sand and stay there for a long time.

Dozens of boats crowd the water, some chugging on a north-south route, others just drifting. I start counting but lose track after forty-five. Every imaginable kind of vessel is out there—even some canoes and kayaks from Mud Bay. Farther down the inlet, almost to the bridge, I spot the bright orange inflatable research raft.

"Pretty amazing, isn't it?" says a voice nearby and I jump.

It's Tal, Dad's boss. He's standing to my left, peering out at the water from under a bright blue cap with the compass logo of Seattle's baseball team. He rocks back and forth on his heels, his hands in the pockets of his hiker shorts. The binoculars hanging around his neck bounce up and down with each move.

"I'd say there's close to fifty boats out there and that's just as far as I can see," he continues, as if I'd answered. "Wouldn't surprise me if it's three times that number on up to Silverdale." He takes off his cap, scratches his almost-bald head, then sets it right again. "What they ought to do is get a National Fisheries patrol boat out here. Keep people in line."

I can't tell if he sees me or he's just talking out loud to himself. Either way, he doesn't seem to care that I don't answer.

"This keeps up, there's gonna be trouble. Couple of years ago, up in the San Juans, I saw a guy try to smack a gray whale with an oar. And another bozo tried bouncing over the back of an orca on a water sled."

Finally, he looks at me and squints.

"I'm flummoxed, so what would that make me?"

"Umm, confused? Or . . . worse than confused. Kind of like, unsure what to do next," I say, glad this one was easy but also grateful for the distraction.

"Sentence?"

"Okay," I pause. "*She was flummoxed by her friend's questions.*"

"Marisa, Marisa, Marisa," Tal says with a grin. "I'm seriously going to have to ramp up the level of difficulty."

Just then, a big gray and white dog ambles down from the row of houses above the beach. He greets Tal like he knows him, his curved tail wagging.

"Is this your dog?" I ask, surprised. I've never seen Tal bring a dog with him down at Mud Bay.

"Yep, this is Mut," he says. "He's quite old. And yes, he's a mutt, but we spell it with one 't' like the Germans do. Not that you'll be writing him any letters." He bends down and tugs at Mut's wiry little beard. "Are you trying to *finagle* something from me, you silly dog?" Tal looks up at me questioningly, but I frown. "One to look up," he says, smiling.

"I always wanted a dog, but my mom is allergic." I bend down to scratch Mut behind his soft ears. "I had a great cat though. Her name was Blackberry. But she got lost when we moved. Or ran away. We're not sure. My dad thinks maybe she got scared and then couldn't find her way back to a new place. Or she might've snuck into somebody's garage and couldn't get out when they closed it."

I'm doing that thing when you're nervous and you talk too much.

"We put up signs. I looked for her for a long time. Now sometimes I forget what it was like having her around at all. . . ."

My voice trails off and an awkward silence settles between us. Why am I telling him all this? It's not even what I'm really feeling, which is that if Mom hadn't left, we'd never have moved and Blackberry would still be around.

"I know what that's like," Tal says, his voice low.

I brush the sand off my jeans and straighten up, surprised. He's listening, taking me seriously. And suddenly, I have an urge to tell Tal everything—about Mom leaving, about how I'm so angry at Dad for not stopping her, how I feel so lost, and how nobody else seems to think any of it is strange. It makes no sense.

"Can I walk Mut sometime?" I ask on a whim.

"Anytime you like," he says. "He needs more walks than he gets."

He cocks his head backwards, toward the row of houses facing the inlet. "We live up there in that monstrosity." I turn to look, and there's no mistaking which house he means.

Rising high up from the sandy beach road is a large three-story Victorian house with two circular turrets, its roof covered in colored shingles, gables facing in all directions. Everybody in town knows this house, not so much for the style but because it's painted purple and white, with a little bit of lilac thrown in for good measure.

"I've seen houses like that," I tell him, which is a pretty lame thing to say.

"Me too!" he laughs, "but they're in San Francisco or Switzerland. It sticks out like a sore thumb here." Tal sighs. "Never would've guessed my wife would want to live in an old Victorian. But you pick your battles."

Looking at the house, I remember the summer we helped our landlord build a fence in front of our house on East Sixteenth Street.

When we finished, Mom and Dad told me I could pick the paint color. I spent hours poring over paint chips and finally picked purple. Somehow, our landlord approved and sure enough, we painted the fence purple. I wonder now if it was because I'd seen this house.

"Fact of the Day," Tal says, turning to me. "The Boeing Aircraft Factory in Everett, Washington, is the largest building in the world, measured in volume. Number one in the world!"

I bend down to offer one last pet to Mut. His grayish fur feels warm from the sun.

"Well, goodness, Marisa, don't you want to know *how many cubic feet?*"

"Sure, Mr. Reese," I grin, "how many?"

"Four hundred and seventy-two million cubic feet of useable space." He shakes his head in awe. "Right in our own backyard."

Finagle. I have to remember to look that one up. And for the first time in a long while, I feel myself smile.

———

I hurry home along the eastern perimeter of the inlet, skirting Lions Field to avoid the crowds, and taking the residential streets instead. Just past the park, I head down toward the water again. The wind has picked up and big puffy clouds blow across the sky. Scenes and conversations from this morning keep coming back to me. I run through them, again and again, like when you're watching a movie and you hit rewind a couple of times to try to figure out what exactly happened in the scene. In my replay, insulting Harris and running from Lena feel wrong now and I have this sudden urge to make them both right.

I'm not really looking where I'm going when I suddenly feel something brush against my leg. I stop, just catching myself from tripping over a rope somebody has strung across the beach road, stretching all the way from the water's edge up to the house that faces the beach. Without thinking much about it, I lift the rope and bend down to scoot under.

"Hey!" a loud voice yells. "Can't you read the sign?"

I look up. It's Grace, wearing sunglasses and a baseball cap with the word *Cruiser*, the name of her father's boat, on it. Her family owns and rents out this whole row of houses. When she sees it's me, she sprints down the front steps of the porch.

"Beach access. Five dollars," she demands, pointing to a handwritten cardboard sign swinging from the rope divider.

I stare at her, not understanding. "What?"

"Five dollars." she repeats. "To cross our beach if you want to see the whales."

I snort. "I'm not here to watch the whales, Grace. I'm on my way to the bridge." Why am I even bothering to explain? I can't believe she has the nerve to try this. "Anyway, you can't charge people to walk on the beach. It's a public right-of-way."

"My dad says that's just a courtesy, " she says, ready with an answer. "Owners can decide whether or not to allow free access. And we're not."

She's standing in front of me now, blocking my way, her hand stretched out like she actually expects me to lay down a five-dollar bill, which is crazy really when you think about it, because Grace's family is one of the richest in the inlet. Lena says her house is huge. Besides these rentals, her father also owns the biggest marina over at Phinney Bay, plus a lumber store on the peninsula. I'm debating how much I want to fight this, when a screen door slams and Grace's father appears on the porch.

"Everything all right?" he calls down.

Grace turns back toward the house with an irritated look. And an uneasy feeling comes creeping up inside me. When the whales first arrived, we treated them like guests. Now, they're just a novelty, something for people to exploit, make money from because of their visit.

Grace is still staring at me, waiting. I force myself to swallow my words as I make a quick about-face and storm off, making sure to kick back as much sand as possible. But I can't shake the feeling that this whole situation is just going to get worse and worse.

CHAPTER 8

I take the long way home, thinking about what a disaster the day has been. Up ahead looms the Warren Avenue Bridge, the larger of the two bridges that cross the Narrows. I sprint up the concrete steps to the walkway and in a millisecond a line of speeding cars buzzes me on the left, their engine noise amplified by the sound of rubber tires on metal. Halfway across, a fender-bender blocks the right lane. A driver speeds by, laying on his horn, making me jump. I pick up my pace and breathe a sigh of relief when I finally reach the other side.

Back home, I kick off my shoes and sink down onto the couch. It feels like days have passed instead of only hours since Dad dropped me off at the inlet. I try to read and do some homework, but after a few feeble attempts I give up. The next sounds I hear are pots clattering and running water. Late afternoon light streams into the window, and the smell of Dad's cooking drifts my way.

"Hey, sleepyhead," Dad says. "Busy day?"

I stretch and rub my eyes as he comes into my line of vision.

Garlic and herbs. The aroma reminds me of all the dinners Dad has cooked since Mom left. I realize I've never offered to help, not even to heat up leftovers. I've let Dad do it all. He probably didn't feel much like cooking either, but he never said a word. I feel such a rush of shame, my eyes fill with tears.

"Marisa?"

Dad sits down next to me on the couch and puts his arm around me, and I lose it. The next minute I'm bawling, crying like a three-year-old and I can't seem to stop. Dad just keeps holding me. Since Mom left, I've felt like one of those razor clams we used to try to rouse out of hiding on our family trips to the coast. The minute you get near, and they sense your touch, they pull in their bodies so quick, it's like they're hiding something.

Finally, I take a deep breath and my tears stop. "Dad?"

"Umm?"

"Don't you miss her?" I whisper. There. I asked it.

He doesn't miss a beat. "Of course I do," he whispers. "You know that, Marisa."

"Is she . . . is she really coming back?"

"I hope so. I think so."

Dad moves even closer. My hands are cold and he starts rubbing them between his warm palms. "There's something you need to know, Marisa."

A rush of fear courses through me. I look at Dad, thinking how I've done my best to avoid reading Mom's letters and now he's going to tell me the worst of it anyway.

"When we married, your mother asked me to promise never to ask about her past. Maybe I shouldn't have agreed, but at the time I was so crazy in love that I didn't think a thing of it. We had our future together and that was all that seemed to matter, not the past."

I stare at Dad, unbelieving.

"You guys . . . never talked about her childhood or anything?"

Dad shakes his head. "I made a promise."

"But . . . that's crazy! Why would she make you promise that?" I pull away, tucking my legs underneath me. Then something dawns on me. "Is *that* why she'd never answer my questions about her parents, or tell me about growing up? I thought it was just me!"

The only reason I even knew Mom had grown up in California was because of all the rain here. She always said she missed the California heat.

Dad leans back and sighs.

"I do know a few stories," he admits, and I wait, holding my breath.

"She grew up in Southern California, somewhere down in the San Gabriel Valley. That you already know. But it wasn't days of California-dreamin' beaches and the Rose Bowl Parade. This was a place with pig sties, car-wrecking plants, and people whose only financial plan in life was hoping to win at the racetrack. Her street dead-ended into a dairy farm, which sounds fun but apparently wasn't. The cows passed their days in pens on cement slabs. When the workers hosed down the cement, rivers of mud and cow dung ran off into her front yard."

Already, this is more than I've ever heard and I have to bite my lip not to interrupt.

"Your grandmother hated living there, and she drank. A lot. I wormed it out of your mother once because it bugged me that she would never take even a sip of wine." He pauses. "I never met either of her parents, but I suspect this isn't about them. This is something else your mother has been running from for a long time."

Dad stops, and I can tell he thinks he's already said too much.

"That's all I know. The stories stop when she gets to high school, and I honored my promise not to ask. We focused on making our own stories, new ones, together."

Dad gets up and walks over to the window facing the inlet.

"Your mom is a keen observer of human nature, Marisa. That's why she's so good at her work. The only person she keeps at arm's length is herself." He turns to me. "Do you understand what I'm saying?"

No! I want to scream, I *don't* understand.

"Why keep everything a secret?" The tears start up again. I try to hold them in but can't. "Did she think people were going to *hate* her or something?" My eyes squeezed shut, I feel Dad moving closer, then the warmth of his arms encircling me again.

"Why do any of us keep a secret?" Dad asks. "Because we're afraid. Once we tell someone the truth, there's no other way but to face it ourselves."

"But it all feels so *wrong*." I can feel my voice rising but can't control it. "She always said it's okay to ask for help," I say, remembering that night outside the shelter. "And then she just left. Why didn't she stay and let us help her?"

I think Dad's going to tell me not to worry but when I open my eyes he's smiling!

"What?" I ask, surprised.

"That's very good thinking, Marisa." He sticks his hands in the pockets of his jeans.

"I think there is a way that you can help her. Think about it. What are letters, if not stories?"

And for some crazy reason my heart leaps. Dad's right. I wipe my eyes and make a decision. Even if it makes no sense, or even if her letters say she committed some horrible crime years ago and the only way I'll ever see her again now is to visit her in jail—

Or even if all she says again is "be good," I make myself a promise.

The next letter Mom sends—I'm reading it.

―――

Sunday morning, I'm the first one down at Lions Field, ready to go. Kevin from the Whale Research Center arrives, and together we load the rafts in silence, as the sky slowly lightens. Finally, other volunteers start trickling in. Standing on the wet wood of the dock, I make Lena wait while I apologize for running off. There's somebody else I need to find too, to make things right, but Lena says Harris never came back yesterday, and I suspect he won't be back today, so that will have to wait until next week.

Just past nine o'clock, we push off from the dock. The morning is breezy and warm, all the early threats of bad weather seem to have blown away.

"Great day for whale watching," Kevin says. He scans the skies, frowning. "Let's hope it clouds over and keeps people home."

Our vessel is called *Wave*. It's one of two twelve-foot-long inflatable research rafts that SoundKeeper has sent to the inlet. *Wave* is bright orange, with two bench seats and a gas motor mounted on the rear that Mr. O'Connor is manning. Once all of us are settled—me, Lena, Kevin, and Naomi, a graduate student working with Kevin—our knees practically touch.

The floor of the raft is cluttered with a megaphone, a couple of hydrophones for listening to the sounds the whales make underwater, radios, backpacks, sacks of SoundKeepers's "Better Boater" flyers to distribute to whale watchers, and water bottles. Flying from a small mast is a yellow flag identifying our craft as a research vessel, which means we're allowed to get closer to the whales.

We motor slowly out, scanning for any sign of the pod. The inlet is already starting to fill up with boaters, and once we clear the shoreline, it's easy to see up and down its whole length. I look to the south, and there in the distance, just entering under the bridge are two big whale watching boats. Lena spots them at the same time I do.

"Whoa! They're humongous," she says. "Remember being on one of those at camp?"

I do remember. It was almost as big as the ferry that runs to Seattle, with two full walk-around upper and lower decks, even a snack bar.

"Any of the cities big enough to send out tour boats like that are at least an hour and a half away," Naomi says, as we all watch the boats steam closer. "The news must be spreading."

Just then a short, sharp whale call rings out close by— *Aiiieeee*—and we hear the unmistakable hissing sound of whales coming up to breathe.

Pfoosh—Pfoosh. Pfoooooshhhhhh.

Lena gasps and I swivel around. There in the water, parallel to our raft, and no more than a hundred yards away, five black, glossy dorsal fins glide by, all at slightly different heights.

Seeing them here, so close, a little thrill runs through me. Then, a *huge* fin—probably five feet high—heads straight toward us! At the last minute the whale dives under, and I can see its black-and-white patterned body glide by just a few feet away. A little ways off, two whales spyhop simultaneously, their heads poking up through the flat calm of the water. A second later they're gone, and when they surface again they're swimming side by side, the head of one pressed against the fluke of the other. We all watch, mesmerized, as each whale raises a pec fin, almost as if in greeting, then rolls and dives in unison.

Then there's a rush of excitement in the boat as everyone suddenly has a job to do.

Mr. O'Connor kills the motor as one of the orcas glides close by again, the exhale of its breath sending a plume of mist rising over the raft. *Pfoosh—Pfooooosh.* The other whales race back and forth. Naomi quickly lowers one of the hydrophones into the water, securing it to the raft. She hits the record button, and the air comes alive with the voices of the orcas. Clicks and pops, whistles, squeals, and screeches echo and roll over us, reverberating in the open air.

"There's my noisy bunch," Naomi says, smiling. "Nice to hear you again."

"That's L57," Kevin announces, peering through binoculars. "Male, nickname Faith, about twenty. His mother died a couple of years ago, so he usually spends time with Canuck and her daughter Lulu. He's a real leader. Let's see. . . ." He scans slowly with the glasses. "Yep, bingo. There they are." He points to a cluster of three whales farther west of us, heading north. "Definitely L-25 sub-pod."

"But . . . how can you tell?" Lena asks, following Kevin's gaze.

Before he can answer, I point at Faith, who's rolling side to side now with another whale.

"See the dorsal fin, and the saddle patch—the grayish white area at the base? Those are like orca fingerprints. Each whale has their own fin shape and saddle patch markings."

Kevin glances my way, surprised to hear my explanation.

"Marisa's our local orca expert," Mr. O'Connor says. "Watch out for her—she'll steal your job, fin-guy!"

Lena grins and I feel my face redden. I think about Muncher, his little round black eye marking. Its placement, there on the very edge of his white oval eye patch, seems just about perfect to me.

"The nicks and scars on their fins help too," Naomi adds. "You train your eye. Pretty soon, it's easy to tell them apart."

I spot another smaller group farther out, swimming around in slow circles, and lean in closer to Kevin.

"Is that normal?" I have to shout to make myself heard over all the calls coming from the hydrophone.

"All behavior is communication. It's probably just that they're in unknown waters," Kevin answers. His camera clicks away furiously. "It's too early to be alarmed, but we'll keep a close watch. They're eating and they seem to be vocalizing normally, so those are good signs."

I have this sudden urge to tell him that eating and talking normally aren't always sure signs that things are okay. But I bite my tongue.

"Okay, y'all, enough chattering," Kevin tells us. "Let's get to work."

For nearly an hour, the orcas stay close. We keep busy recording their sounds, taking pictures, noting all the individual whales we can identify. But whenever one breaches or spyhops, all work stops. The thrill of each new sighting is as spectacular as the first. When one whale makes a move—a cartwheel, a tail or pec slap—sure enough the rest will mimic the same routine, as if they have a choreographed dance all planned out.

Several times, we see a few adults with calves go chasing at the surface, drawn by a cluster of chum salmon, their backs and dorsal fins slicing through the water together in a tight group.

"Watching orcas chase fish only gives a hint of what's going on underneath the water," Kevin tells us. "They'll surround the fish with rings of bubbles, then take turns diving beneath the school and looping around. It's like an orca carousel," he explains, "with dozens of fish being shoveled up into their enormous jaws."

"Watching them hunt is one of my favorite things," Naomi adds. "You can just sense their joy and cunning, their love of the open ocean and of hunting with the group."

As if the most important thing is just being part of the group.

For the rest of the day, we motor around the inlet, passing out leaflets to boaters outlining SoundKeeper's whale watching guidelines: stay at least 200 yards away from the whales; if they move toward your boat, kill your engine; if they head south out of the inlet, stay behind and don't cut off their line of travel.

"That's the most important one," Kevin explains. "They'll need a straight shot out when they want it." Red and green flashes glimmer in the water—the colors of chum salmon—a sign that the whales are foraging again. "And let's hope they make their exit soon, before the food runs out."

It's getting cold now on the water. Listening to Kevin, I shiver and try to remember how many salmon a full-grown orca needs to eat every day. Twenty? Maybe twenty-five? Even though Dyes Inlet always seems chock-full of fish, salmon runs are down this year.

And now we've got nineteen whales here. I do some quick math. That's a lot of salmon—almost 500 a day! Even worse, it's late in the season, when most chum have already made their runs back home to Chico Creek.

Will the fish run out before the whales leave? I don't think anybody knows the answer, not even Kevin. And I don't want to even think about what will happen if they do.

But it's too late. Now I've got one more thing to worry about.

CHAPTER 9

Orca Day 8

After the first whale weekend, we fall into a rhythm and the days pass in a busy blur. Since we're helping with the SoundKeeper program, we're excused from school at noon. We grab a quick lunch, then head down to where Kevin has set up his headquarters at Lions Field.

Two days in a row, I detour over to the post office. Now that I'm expecting—*hoping*—for a letter from Mom, there's nothing. Just junk mail and bills.

Everybody keeps expecting the whales to leave, too. But they don't, and after more than a week, Kevin seems a little more nervous each day. On Wednesday, with orca fever still running high, I navigate through the lunchtime crowd to my locker. When I slam the door shut and look up, Harris is standing right in front of me. For two days straight, I've been trying to find him, but now it takes all my courage not to look away.

"Harris, hi . . . how's it going?" Nothing. I clutch my books tight to my chest and take a deep breath. "Look . . . what happened on Saturday . . . I'm sorry. I don't know why I said what I did. What you do isn't any of my business."

The minute the words are out of my mouth I know they sound wrong—like I don't care.

Harris drops his eyes to the floor. "Whatever," he mumbles.

"I'm biking down to Lions Field," I blurt out. "Want to come? We just hang out and answer questions."

"Can't do that," he says, crouching down to shove some crumbled papers into his backpack. "Don't know nothing about whales."

He's being so hard, and I feel a flash of anger, until I remember how easy it is to get to that place.

"You sure?"

"Yep," he says, but doesn't leave.

I ask about Jesse, thinking this will be my way in but instead, a cloud passes over his dark eyes and I know I've upset him again.

"Everything's the same. Nothing ever changes." He slings his backpack over his shoulder and brushes past me, fast. "I gotta go. See ya."

I want to make it better somehow, but I've got no clue how to begin. Then, a second later I hear his voice again.

"Hey . . . whales still there?"

"Yeah, they are," I say, turning around, smiling. "It's amazing! They're—" But he's already gone, and I'm left standing there, talking to myself.

———

Biking down to Lions Field I'm glad to have a job to do, even if it's only sitting at a table and handing out a sheet of rules. *All behavior is communication*, Kevin says. And it looks like I've just had another screwed up one with Harris.

"Do you know what somebody just asked me?" Lena calls out first thing when I arrive. "Could they maybe put on a wet suit and *swim* with the whales?" She rolls her eyes in disbelief. "Please, send me out there," she points to the blue water of the inlet, "where there's *intelligent* life."

We laugh and decide on the spot to keep a list of visitors' craziest questions. Then we get to work and spend the next hour explaining breaching, the differences in dorsal fins, L Pod's genealogy, and how you can tell who's who by the way the whales group themselves when they swim.

"The oldest female will always swim in the center of the pod, closest to the youngest calves," I tell a visitor. "The adult daughters stay on the outside ring until they have their own babies. Then sometimes they'll travel separately, but they're always considered part of the pod."

As I talk, I'm painfully aware that I wouldn't know any of this except for Mom. Besides our annual fall trip up to the San Juans, some springs Mom also tried to squeeze in a "Welcome the Whales Home" visit in the spring when the pods start arriving back from their travels up and down the coast. Everything I know about orcas I learned on those trips. Everything.

"Marisa, you okay?" Lena touches me on the arm.

I nod, wondering if I'll ever have the chance to take another one of those trips, when suddenly there's a huge commotion. Kevin and Naomi come racing down the path toward the shoreline. Something's happening—something big.

"What's going on?" Lena shouts as they pass.

"They're heading out!" Naomi calls back over her shoulder.

Lena and I exchange excited glances—the whales! Without a word we race to follow. When Kevin reaches the water's edge, he keeps running until the water is sloshing around his ankles. Close behind on his heels, Naomi is speaking into her radio, her voice rapid and tense. I strain to hear but can't make out what she's saying.

Then Kevin brings the white megaphone up and his amplified voice booms out over the water.

"ATTENTION, VESSELS. DO NOT APPROACH THE WHALES. REPEAT. ALL VESSELS KEEP YOUR DISTANCE AND STAY BEHIND THE WHALES."

Beyond the crush of people crowding the dock, what I can see now on the water makes my heart skip a beat. The pod is swimming fast, dead center in the inlet, heading south toward the Narrows. Behind, chasing them, is a mass of boats of every shape and size. Orcas can swim close to thirty miles an hour out in open water, but in a small bay like this they're no match against an outboard motorboat. Even from this distance, I can already tell some of the boats are gaining.

Naomi clicks off her radio and clips it back on her belt. "Apparently, there's no Coast Guard boat anywhere near here."

"I placed that request *days* ago," Kevin barks. He booms out his warning again but the boaters ignore it. Some have shot ahead now, and are running on a parallel path with the pod.

He turns to Naomi. "You say the Port Washington police are on the bridge?"

"I think so. They must be by now," she says nervously, looking in the direction of the bridge. "They deployed two squad cars but I can't raise them on the radio to confirm."

"The van is back at the marina and all our rafts are out." Kevin looks around frantically. "Damn! I've got to get somebody out to that bridge! We have to head them off."

"Aw, man," Lena whispers, shooting me a worried look. We're both rooted to the spot, unsure what to do next. The whales are far past our line of vision now, but we can see clearly the flotilla of boats still in pursuit. The acrid smell of diesel fuel from their wake drifts toward the shore, nauseating me. I remember a trick Dad taught me and breathe out quickly several times trying to clear my head so I can think.

Three days ago, I made the trip from almost this exact spot to the Warren Avenue Bridge on foot. Today I have my bike.

"Mr. Brooks?" My voice sounds distant on the noisy dock. "I can bike to the bridge."

Kevin looks right at me and for a split second I know exactly what he's thinking—*a twelve-year-old girl?* But he allows himself just one quick glance toward the water before he shouts, "GO!" And in an instant, almost as if his word was the blessing I'd been waiting for, I spring to life.

"Tell the police we sent you," Naomi yells, tossing me her ID pass.

"Tell them they've got to clear the Narrows!" Kevin orders. "I don't want any boat traffic anywhere near that passage. None. The whales need to have a clear shot out under the bridge to the outer bay!"

I tuck Naomi's pass into my back pocket, turn, and race to get my bike. Any hesitation I might have had is gone. My mind and body feel in perfect harmony. As I pedal off, I know exactly what I need to do.

———

I'm not afraid to ride my bike fast. Mom used to say I scared the daylights out of her when she saw me riding down the hill near our house. But today, I bike faster than I ever have before. I ride so fast I'm afraid I'll lose control if my concentration breaks, so I focus on keeping my feet pumping in circles—*up and down, up and down*—the rhythm matching the beating of my heart.

Somehow, I keep it up. And all the while, I can hear the continued calls Kevin is sending out over the water. From this distance, the sound is almost musical, and reminds me of the orcas' vocalizations. Without hearing the words, you'd never know it's really a desperate call to save the orcas. I ride on, wondering if the boaters will keep ignoring it.

I reach the stairs that ascend to the bridge and skid my bike to a stop, throwing it aside. Panting, I climb up to the bridge deck and sprint along the side walkway to where two Port Washington patrol cars are parked.

"Hello! Excuse me . . . please!" I bully my way in to get the attention of the officers. "I'm with the whales . . . I mean . . . the whale researchers. They need you to clear the Narrows!" I pull out Naomi's ID pass allowing unrestricted access to county services. "It's the whales . . . they're coming . . . they want you to keep the boats away from the bridge passage so the whales can get out!"

I must look half-crazy or maybe the officer really understands what I'm trying to say, but all that matters is that, in the heat of the moment, he believes me. He grabs the patrol car's radio mike and together we run to the north bridge wall that overlooks the entrance to the inlet.

"THIS IS THE PORT WASHINGTON POLICE. MARINE VESSELS . . . MOVE TO THE PERIMETER. CLEAR THE WATERWAY IMMEDIATELY. REPEAT. ALL MARINE VESSELS CLEAR THE WATERWAY. THIS IS THE PORT WASHINGTON POLICE. . . ."

The call to clear the passage rings in my ears as the officer broadcasts the order again and again out over the water. All the traffic on the bridge is pretty much stopped now as people pour out of their cars to peer over the wall, trying to see what's causing the disruption.

Boats of all shapes and sizes are clustered around a center

space that must be the pod. They're close now, maybe 300 yards from the bridge, approaching steadily.

They're so close—almost out!

C'mon. C'mon! I chant to myself.

I hold my breath and allow myself to think they're going to make it, when suddenly, the scream of an outboard motor rips through the air. A speedboat comes into view, flanking the pod on the west side, tracing a wide arc to the east. It accelerates with a tremendous roar, and passes directly in front of the whales, cutting them off. It all happens so fast it seems unreal. Standing on the bridge, I'm helpless to do anything but watch.

In the water below, the whales' reaction is much the same. The pod stops dead in its tracks and the sound of their exhalations fills the air.

Pfoosh—Pfoosh—Pfooshhhhh. A massive spouting of water and mist rises up everywhere, almost to where I'm standing. I breathe in its distinctive odor—musty and rich. Some of the animals surface and exhale, then dive again. At my elbow, the police officer is repeating his call to clear the area. But it's too late. We watch in horror as the same motorboat reverses its course and speeds again in front of the whales, crossing now in the opposite direction.

I spot two orcas, young ones, circling, right below me. Right below the bridge. I strain to see their saddle patches. One is Muncher, I just know it. Is he all right? What are they doing?

Two larger whales approach, mothers maybe, and I watch as they do something I've never seen before in all my years of whale watching. Both adults lift their tails straight up into the air, keeping their heads and blowholes under the water. Then together, they bring their tails down hard, slapping their flukes on the surface of the water. Once, twice, three times—*Smack! Smack! Smack!*

The noise, so close, carried up to the bridge deck, is deafening. Then the huge female in the center of the pod humps her back, facing away from the bridge, and makes a deep dive. One by one the others follow, until the water between the two lines of boats is churning and rippling below, but empty at the surface. I shut my eyes for a minute, hoping for a miracle, but when I open them again, Muncher and the other calf have turned back toward the inlet, and I watch as nineteen whales swim very slowly away from the Warren Avenue Bridge, back into Dyes Inlet.

————

The frenzied activity continues all around me, but I can't seem to stop staring at the empty water below. From my spot on the bridge, I can see down the whole of the inlet—it's a spectacular view. People are chattering and going about their business again, as if nothing unusual has happened. Maybe it hasn't, for them. They were here just to watch the whales, not bothering to really *see*, not understanding how important it is for the pod—for Muncher—to leave the inlet and make it safely back home. It makes me so angry, thinking about it, that I kick my sneaker toe again and again against the deck railing.

And what about me? I think about Mom and Harris and how hard it is to understand what makes people do what they do or act a certain way. Maybe I'm no different either from those people in their boats. If I'm really honest, I have to admit that lately I haven't been very willing to take the time to figure out why people do what they do, or to think about how everything is connected.

I know I should leave and ride back to Lions Field, but I can't seem to pull myself away from the railing. The pod is far down the inlet now, split into smaller groups and swimming in slow circles. I strain to see if I can locate Muncher, but they're too far away.

Below me, the water that was churning and gurgling furiously only minutes ago is calm now, as if nothing had ever disturbed it. Naomi told us a story the other day. Whales, she said, never exclude anyone from their pod. It doesn't matter if they're weak or injured or just different. In the world of the orca, everyone is a part of the group. Harris would probably say they "get it."

Nineteen whales. I wonder if they know what just happened.

I hope they know that some of us won't stop fighting to get them home.

CHAPTER 10

Orca Day 9

You did everything you could, Marisa," Naomi reminds me again and again, "even more." But it's no good. After my failed attempt to clear the Narrows, I feel miserable. And that's when I make my decision. Maybe I couldn't get Mom to stay, and I don't know if I'll get the chance to convince her to come back. But no matter what it takes, I'm determined to help the whales find their way home.

And I'm not alone. The whole mood at Lions Field has changed.

"No more playing nice," Kevin announces. "We need a constant presence on the water." He starts parking his orange and white VW van at the dock, working extra late, the opera music he loves drifting out into the night air. Rumor has it that yesterday he slept in the van, then drove this morning over to the county sheriff and Port Washington police department office and stormed in, demanding state and federal patrols on Dyes Inlet for as long as necessary.

I want to ask Kevin about Muncher's mother and the other whale near the bridge, about why they lifted their tails high into the air and smacked them down. I want to know what it means. But everyone's too busy, so I make a mental note to ask later, when things calm down.

To be extra safe, Kevin puts out a call for private boaters to lend their vessels to SoundKeeper. Tal Reese offers five of his motorboats and workers to go along, and Dad arranges for me to cross with Tal to deliver the first of the boats to Mud Bay this afternoon.

"Hello again, Marisa!" Tal greets me. He arrives at the field wearing his Mariners cap, plus a waterproof anorak and waders. This time, a whistle's also been added to the binoculars dangling from his neck.

I glance down, looking for Mut. Tal notices and smiles.

"No, he's a bit too much of a senior dog to handle all this excitement. So what have you got for me?" He scans our sheet of whale watching guidelines. "You know, you should add that to your list—Leave Pets at Home. Dogs seem to get rattled around whales. Not to mention their barking doesn't add to the calm."

"They'd ruin the 'tranquillity' of the experience!'" I tell Tal, proud of my vocabulary.

"Excellent, Marisa," Tal says, winking.

While Tal prepares one of the three motorboats he keeps at the Lions Field marina, I gather a thick stack of SoundKeeper flyers and wait. It's strange to think how the whales control everyone's schedule now. Tracking how long they've been here is how I've started to measure my days.

Nine days and counting. Tomorrow is already Halloween, one of my favorite holidays. Dad's too, but not Mom's. She hated dressing up—too much fuss and bother she said—but she always loved watching us prepare.

Our best year was the time we decided to be sea creatures. I was a starfish and Dad was a clam. He stole the idea from a local restaurant that uses a walking clam in their advertising and it worked. We won first prize in the annual Silverdale Halloween parade. This year, there's been no time for costumes but Dad promises he'll keep tomorrow afternoon free for the parade.

When Tal is ready, I climb in the boat and we set off from the dock, heading southwest toward the marina. It's been warm but now a thick wall of blue-black clouds moves quickly in over the inlet and I shiver in the chilly air. Seagulls swoop and caw, diving to grab a bite. After days of activity, the inlet is eerily empty of boaters. The only other craft in sight is a canoe over near the west shore, heading south.

"They've been hanging out further north," he says, scanning in all directions looking for any sign of the whales, but I see him shake his head. It's strange how such huge creatures can be so hard to find.

"I'm not surprised, Chico Creek's their meal ticket. That creek was what sold me on living here," Tal says. "You can't beat the fishing."

"You didn't grow up here?"

"Nope, but Bette did, my wife. But I've *acclimated*."

He says the last word slowly. I look over at him and sigh, but this one I can figure out from the way he used it in the sentence.

"To get used to something," I tell Tal.

He laughs and nods his head. "But to answer your question, I'm from Ohio. Moved here in '62 to take a job at Boeing. Loved airplanes and boats. Have I mentioned that the Boeing plant up in Everett is the largest building—"

"Yes!"

"Okay, okay, just one more and I'll give you a break," he says and I grin. "Let's see . . . how about a little local history. When Bette and I first moved here, it was before they built our lovely Warren Avenue Bridge. The only way to get from east to west Port Washington was to drive all the way north around the top of the inlet past Silverdale. Which is why, of course, I bought my first boat."

As he talks, his eyes stay glued tight to the binoculars. After multiple sweeps to be sure he's not missing anything, he lowers the glasses.

"I'm guessing you're one of that rare breed, a Northwest native."

I laugh and nod yes, thinking how I've always known I want to stay here forever.

"Your kids must be natives, too," I tell him. I don't actually know if Tal has kids, but he seems like a dad.

"That's true. . . ."

Overhead a seagull circles around us, screeching. Tal cranes his head up to look and something passes over his face, some cloud of a memory, but in a second it's gone. "Is your mom helping out with the whales, too?" he asks.

I shift uncomfortably in my seat. "Umm . . . my mom's traveling right now," I answer, which isn't really a lie. I haven't spoken about her out loud for so long that my own words startle me. I can't help thinking that if Mom were here, she would have already figured out how to get the whales home. To my surprise, the thought makes me feel proud, not sad.

"Traveling, eh?" Tal says. "One of life's best pursuits . . . gives you perspective."

That tells me that Dad hasn't told Tal the real story.

"Let me show you what you're supposed to do," I say, changing the subject before he asks for more details.

In the ten minutes it takes me to explain the SoundKeeper guidelines, there's a massive change in the weather. Those dark clouds I saw earlier sweep in to cover the whole sky and the wind picks up something fierce. We're less than a half mile off the west shore now, and strong waves are splashing across our bow.

Tal maneuvers the motorboat across the wide expanse of the inlet, keeping the wind behind us, and when I turn, its force takes my breath away. Up ahead, I can see the canoe I noticed earlier struggling, turned sideways to the wind and waves. Even in the darkening light, I can tell from the markings that it's one of Tal's boats, from Mud Bay. This is really odd, because all Dad's rentals are due back at four o'clock on weekdays.

It must be past four by now. I glance down at my watch to double-check the time. It can't be more than a second that I take my eyes off the water, but when I look up again—the canoe is gone! It was right there, directly in my line of vision, I'm sure of it. I scan quickly from left and right, and spot it, flipped over in the water not far from its original location.

"Mr. Reese!" I yell, pointing into the wind. "Look!"

Tal grabs for his binoculars. I squint hard but it's raining now, and I can't see any sign of the paddlers.

"I see them!" Tal exclaims. I can barely make out two heads bobbing in the water near the rim of the overturned craft. In an instant, we're speeding in their direction.

"Hang on!" he shouts to me over the revving of the motor. We race toward the pair as quickly as we safely can but even then it'll take us a good minute or two.

Before I was even ten years old, Dad warned me about salt-water canoeing. It's different and tricky, even in good weather. If there's a squall, you'd better be an experienced seaman to be out on the inlet. This time of year the water is frigid. We've got to get them out fast or their body temperature will start to drop and they'll go hypothermic.

Tal slows the boat and throws a line overboard before we're even close enough to reach, positioning us carefully to approach the

capsized canoe in a parallel path. But something else seems wrong...
they're awfully low in the water. With a flash of understanding I turn
to Tal, frightened, but he already knows.

"Oh Lord, no life jackets," he mutters under his breath.
One of the first things you learn when you live by the water is
to have a healthy fear of it. No life jackets could mean big trouble.
But how could this be? Dad makes sure everyone—*everyone*, even if
they tell him they're an Olympic swimmer—wears a life jacket when
they rent his boats. I move to the side and lean over, totally unpre-
pared for what I see when I look down. There, clinging to the tie line
and shivering in the ice-cold water, are Harris and Jesse.

———

"Marisa!" Tal yells, "over here ... help me with these!"
I hurry to help him release the life preservers and together we
quickly throw one, then another into the water. With Jesse huddled
close, Harris lunges for the life preserver and manages to wrap one
arm through. It's enough.

"Hold this rope ... tight."
I grip the rope and will myself not to let go, as Tal struggles to
haul Harris and Jesse out of the freezing water and into our boat.
I follow Tal's instructions as quickly as I can, helping to get them
seated and resting in the corner. Both are conscious, but so numb
from the cold, they're like dead weight. Harris mumbles something
we can't make out. I can tell Jesse wants to cry but his freezing body
won't let him.

Tal bends over each of them and to my relief, finds a pulse on
both.

"They're pretty well chilled," he says, punching a few buttons on
his radio. "Bette? I'm bringing in two that we just fished out of the inlet.
Yeah. Pulse is pretty regular, but we'll need a Medic-van at the dock."

He clicks off the radio. "My wife. She works intake at Evanston."

I pull two Mylar blankets from the boat's emergency kit, and cover Harris and Jesse as well as I can, tucking them in tight, hoping it helps keep out the added chill in the air. There isn't much more we can do now except motor as fast as possible across the inlet.

"All right, folks. Let's get these seals out of the harbor. I knew we had whales visiting, but I haven't seen seals this big since I was in the navy!" He glances my way and grins.

Tal's handling of the situation calms me, but I can tell he's scared too, especially for Jesse. As we race across the water, the crazy string of connections that brought us to this point swirls in my head. Glancing behind, I can see the canoe drifting, getting smaller and smaller in the distance.

I kneel down close to Harris. "Why were you out in one of Dad's canoes," I whisper, mostly to myself, "during a squall, with no life jackets? Why?"

His eyes twitch back and forth, and I know it's useless. All my questions will have to wait. The main thing now is to get them quickly and safely to the hospital.

CHAPTER 11

Jesse won't allow anyone to pull him away from Harris, so the Evanston Urgent Care staff agrees to take them both into the exam room together. Once they're in safe hands, my relief turns to anger. What did he think he was doing out there? Especially taking Jesse with him. I want to shake Harris silly, until an awful thought occurs to me. Was it my fault what happened today? It was *me* who stopped Harris from going out on the inlet that first day.

Evanston's the only medical center for the whole region and it sits chock-a-block on a hill overlooking the inlet. It feels weird being here now, where Mom used to work. I look down at my hands, and I'm surprised to see them shaking. Tal's wife, Bette, notices. She leans over me, wrapping her fingers gently around my wrist to take a pulse.

"What about you, honey?" she asks. "Are you okay?"

Bette has short black hair and kind eyes. A round silver pendant designed in the Northwest Coast Salish style dangles from a short chain around her neck. As she examines me, I study it—the howling face of a wolf silhouetted against the moon. Studying the intricate stamped pattern soothes me. How clever the artist was to depict the moon as an empty space cut out of the silver circle. By taking something away, he gave it meaning.

"She was pretty solid," I hear Tal say. "I couldn't have managed without her."

Despite everything, his words make me feel better. Bette leads me to a cushy red chair near a window and I sink into it, wanting to believe him. Tal hands me a soda and I sip the fizzy drink gratefully. As I watch Bette working, it occurs to me there's a good chance that she knows Mom. Just as I'm about to ask, she turns to Tal.

"Any idea who they are?" she asks, settling down behind her desk and pulling out some papers. Tal starts to shake his head no but I interrupt.

"Harris and Jesse Williams."

"You *know* these two?" Tal says.

"Kind of." I shrug. "He goes to my school, Harris, the older one."

"Do you have a parent's name or number?" Bette asks.

I shake my head. "Their dad's not around a lot . . . he kind of comes and goes. No one's ever seen their mother."

"They're not runaways, are they?" Bette asks in a worried voice.

"No . . . they've been like this since—" I'm about to say *since my mom came home one day about five years ago and told us about two brothers who were coming to the shelter on a regular basis, and she was going to see what she could do about it,* but that seems like an awful lot.

Tal and Bette exchange a quick look and something passes between them that I can't quite read. It never even crossed my mind to tell Tal I knew Harris and Jesse. Now, I wonder why.

Bette reaches for the inlet directory. "Where do they live? I can try to locate the father."

"I . . . I'm not sure . . . a trailer park on the west side of the bridge, I think. . . ." I hesitate. "I don't know where exactly."

"Would your father know?"

Again I have to shake my head no. Mom would, though.

"Who takes care of these kids then?" Tal asks, a little too loudly.

"Hon, it happens all the time," Bette says softly.

Frustrated, Tal gives an exasperated sigh. "Anything else we should know, Marisa?"

I hesitate. "Well . . . Jesse, the younger one, has some trouble learning things, but I don't know what it is exactly. Harris takes really good care of him. . . ." Then I remember Harris took Jesse out on the inlet without a life jacket, ". . . usually."

By now, I'm pretty sure I'm doing more harm than good. I seem to have a talent for that lately. Feeling useless, I sit and watch quietly while Bette makes a few phone calls and fills out forms.

"Will they be okay?" I finally whisper.

Bette answers like Mom would, without stopping her work. "They never lost consciousness," she says. "That's a good thing. Critical for recovery."

Then the automatic doors from the exam rooms swing open and a nurse pokes her head out. "You can come in now if you like."

In the examining room, Jesse is sitting quiet in a wheelchair, another nurse at his side holding his hand. Harris looks pale and weak, but mostly like himself.

"They're going to be fine," the nurse sitting with Jesse tells us. "The doctor's ordered warmed fluids intravenously and we'd like to keep them overnight for observation." He leans over to retrieve his stethoscope from Jesse's grasp. "If they're doing okay after eight hours, they can go home. All we'd recommend is a follow-up evaluation."

Then the doctor enters. "Have you located the parents?" she asks and Bette and Tal move off to the side, to talk together quietly.

I bend down and give Jesse a hug, then walk over to Harris who's sitting slumped on the examining table. I'm so relieved they're both going to be all right that I'm not really angry anymore, just a little disappointed. I'm certain Harris took the canoe from Mud Bay without permission. And Harris knows I know. Then again, who am I to judge? I'd only be pretending if I said I knew what life was like for Harris growing up.

A few uncomfortable minutes pass. I watch as Harris sits fiddling with the strings on his hospital gown.

"I didn't steal it, Marisa," he says, his voice soft but firm. Just like that, without my even asking. "That's the truth. I was gonna bring it back. I was just borrowing it to show Jesse the whales."

I nod slowly, thinking about what I want to say next. "I believe you," I tell him, and the moment I say it I know it's the truth. Surprised, he lifts his head. "The thing is, next time . . . maybe you should borrow life jackets, too."

When he sees me smiling, he grins back.

"Anyways, I guess they had their own plans," he says, and I know he means the whales. "'Cause there was *nothing* going on out there." There's a minute of not-too-uncomfortable silence, then Harris shifts on the table, leaning toward me. "You know, when my old man was still with my mom, sometimes they'd get into this argument, same one all the time, about which of them was stronger, which one of them had done more for me and Jes." He laughs roughly. "Neither one did, really. They were both just making a lot of noise."

Harris never talks this way, so I listen quietly.

"Then you got something super strong, like the orca whale.

No yelling. No screaming. They got nothing to prove. Just swimming around down there in the dark water. One time I got this book for Jes from the library . . . stories and stuff about orcas. Some folks think catching sight of one is kind of lucky, a good omen. That's why I wanted to see them, you know?" He pauses. "One story called the orca 'hunter of the sea.' Said if he ever came back to live on the land again, he'd transform into a wolf! Can you believe that?" He looks at me closely, his eyes bright. "You know whales, Marisa. You think that story's true?"

I think about how Mom tried to help Harris believe his own story, not the ones other people had already made up about him. Who's to say what's true and what's not? I decide even if that orca story isn't actual fact, it's still true.

I nod my head. "Yeah, I think I do."

"That's good. . . ." Harris says, breaking into a wide grin. "So do I."

———

"Be good."

Mom's last words, written just above her name in the letter she left. Just two little words, but everything that's been happening with the whales—and now with Harris—has me thinking about what being "good" means. Does it mean doing what's good for you, or for others? And what about the rest of the creatures on the planet? The cutoff at the bridge sure wasn't good for the whales but I bet it was good for somebody in that speedboat who got a spectacular photograph.

Mom is *so* good at being good. She works so hard to take care of everybody that Dad and I kidded her about it sometimes.

"What about *us*?" we'd whine until we made her laugh.

Once, when I was in sixth grade, we were late leaving the

house for some school event—I can't remember what it was now—but we were rushing around like crazy. Just as we shut the door, a hawk dived into our yard and a huge swarm of smaller birds in the surrounding trees flew off in every direction. We could hear their cries all around. Then there was a loud *thunk* and we saw that a frightened robin had slammed against our big front window, mistaking it for an escape route. The robin had knocked itself silly. I can still see it—wings askew—struggling to stand on the cold ground.

"Oh, goodness," Mom said, watching, "it's going to be easy prey now. We've got to help it."

"Mom!" I protested, "we've got to go. We're so late!"

She didn't even bother to answer.

"Go inside and get a towel, Marisa. Hurry."

When I came back with the towel, she was kneeling near the stunned bird that was shivering now from heat loss.

"Spread it here," she said, patting the ground beside her. As much as I wanted to go, I watched in awe as she reached for the robin and folded its wings gently over its body back into their natural position. Then—like this was something she did every day—she picked up the bird and placed it on the towel, wrapping it loosely several times so that it couldn't escape.

"What are you going to do now?" I asked in a thin voice.

"It just needs a little time to recover its wits." She picked the little bundle up and carried it to the porch, then settled herself on the swing. I stood rooted to the spot, worried we'd never get out of the house. After about fifteen minutes, she gently unwrapped the bird. In an instant, before I could even fully focus, the robin flew off from her hands, totally recovered.

"Okay," she said as if nothing much had happened, "I'm ready to go now."

When Dad comes to pick me up from the hospital, he grills me about Harris.

"Mom always said he was a good kid, he just needed more support," Dad says and I can't help but notice his choice of words. He'd discovered a canoe missing at the marina when he did his final count at closing time. That's when he started calling around, worried whoever had taken it might've gotten into trouble. Finally, he reached the hospital and Bette told him what happened. Imagine his surprise. "I hope I'm making the right decision not pressing charges."

"Dad . . . it's okay," I say, doing my best to reassure him. "They're going to be fine, and you got the canoe back. Nothing bad really happened."

"But it could have, Marisa. Easily. What Harris did wasn't just illegal, it was dangerous."

"I know. But . . . he did it because he wanted to see the whales. He had no other way, nobody to ask—" I stop, another fresh wave of guilt washing over me. "And he's going to work with me and Lena helping out SoundKeeper to make up for it." I make that part up on the spot, but I know Harris will agree. Then another idea pops into my head. "Maybe they can come with us tomorrow afternoon to the parade in Silverdale."

Dad gives me a quizzical look.

"I don't know," I shrug. "Maybe you guys could *talk* or something."

"Good idea," Dad finally agrees, and I breathe a sigh of relief. I have no way of knowing if what I'm saying is true. But after listening to Harris talk in the hospital room, I know something for sure: Harris didn't just *want* to see the whales. He *needed* to see them. Because seeing them up close proves, beyond any shred of doubt, that there's still good in the world. Whales, if they wanted to, could easily kill you. But they don't. They choose another path.

Harris and Jesse could use a little good in their lives. They need to see the whales.

And I think I can help make that happen.

CHAPTER 12

Orca Day 10: Halloween

They can't locate Harris and Jesse's parents or guardians," Dad tells me the next morning, hanging up the phone. "Bette and Tal will be taking them home for the time being."

"Can they do that?" I rub my eyes, surprised. It's almost eleven o'clock. We'd both slept in late after the long night at the hospital and Dad said it was okay if I skipped the only class I have Friday mornings.

Dad gives a short laugh. "Let's just say the hospital looks the other way. Your mother once told me that nurses do it all the time when parents are scarce. Sometimes it's the only way to get them the services they need."

Then the phone rings again, and before I can really register what's happening, Dad's holding it out toward me. "It's Mom. She'd like to talk to you."

For a second, I freeze. Dad keeps holding the phone out, like some kind of life preserver. I grab it and slip onto the stool at the counter.

"Hello?"

"M? Honey, I'm so glad you're there!" There's a pause. Her

voice . . . it sounds so close, like she's right here in the room with me again. I can feel a tightness start up in my chest. I've missed her *so much*.

"Guess where I am?" Still, I don't answer. I can't, my thoughts are all muddled, but she plows ahead anyway. "Azusa, California! My favorite town growing up, I think I told you about it once. They have this sign when you enter, *Everything from A to Z in the*—"

"Mom . . . did Dad tell you about the whales?" I interrupt her. Dad nods at me, then quietly leaves the kitchen. "There are nineteen of them, Mom, *here* in the inlet! And Muncher . . . I'm pretty sure he's here, too." I wait for her reaction, but there's only silence on the other end of the line, so I plow ahead too. "But . . . I'm starting to wonder if they're lost . . . or stuck."

"I wish I could be there to see them with you, M. You know I've loved those whales since the first day I moved to the Northwest. But . . . " she stops, "right now's not a good time, honey. Something happened a long time ago, something I've been avoiding for a long time—"

"Yeah, I know." I can hear my voice starting to waver, not quite so certain anymore. "That's what you said in your letter. But, Mom . . . it's *our* whales. And they need our help! Can't you come home now? You know so much about them—"

"I can't, M," Mom stops my rush of words. Her voice is flat. "Not yet. There's someone important here I need to meet . . . and, well, I'm still working myself up to it."

My throat tightens up. Tears are seconds away.

"Mom . . . I *need* you to come home."

"Honey, listen," I hear Mom say. "I have to go. I've saved up all my quarters, to feed them into the pay phone, but I'm running out. I'll call or write again soon—"

But it's too late. My tears have dried and something else is slowly rising up inside me, taking its place. Mom said no. I'd never imagined that if I flat out asked her to come home, she'd say no. It kind of takes my breath away.

Quickly, I press down on the OFF button, hard, holding it there for a long time. I'm so mad I can feel my body shaking.

When I finally lift my finger, the dial tone blares in my ear.

———

After Mom's call, I work really hard not to go back to worrying and feeling sorry for myself. As we get ready to drive to Evanston Memorial to pick up Harris and Jesse, I keep wondering what's the point of being so capable and strong? Maybe if I was more like Harris—the kind of kid who *needs* Mom's help—things would be different. Those kids seem to have one big advantage. They get Mom's attention.

I tell myself that's just crazy thinking. But it hurts just the same.

———

The annual Silverdale Halloween Parade always draws a big crowd. The only other time all the inlet towns organize an event together is in July, for the whaling festival. Then it's mostly fireworks and food stands, with the big event a rubber duck race on the inlet. Now, here it is almost November, and we've got nineteen real whales swimming around.

Silverdale sits at the uppermost point of Dyes Inlet, just north of Chico Creek and its big salmon runs. When I was little, it was one of my favorite places because of the big seawall embankment near the marina. I could play for hours on that sloping seawall. The sandy beach seemed to be made entirely of bleached bits of pure white shells. I loved the great crunching sounds they made when you walked on them.

Sometimes we'd hike to the interpretive center where there are displays about the history of the area and the Suquamish, the people who have lived here longer than anyone. In the Lushootseed language, *sáq'ad* means "to spear it." The Suquamish called this whole area Sáq'ad, not just Dyes Inlet, but the creek, the estuary, and the camping grounds too, because of all the salmon, oysters, clams, berries, even deer. Whenever we went, I'd spend the whole time imagining what life must have been like here a hundred years ago.

We're halfway to Silverdale when Harris finally speaks up.

"I was planning on returning the canoe when we were done." His eyes are fixed on the landscape outside the car window, but I know he's really talking to Dad. "I should never have borrowed it without asking in the first place. Sometimes I do stupid things, I guess . . . at least that's what people always say."

"Thank you, Harris," Dad says stiffly, but I see his shoulders relax just a little. "I appreciate that."

The mood in the car shifts, just a little. Harris swivels around to look at me, and smiles.

"Except your mom."

"She spent a lot of time with you guys, didn't she?" I ask.

"Yep," Harris nods. "I remember once, she convinced my old man to let her take Jesse to the clinic for some kind of special tests. Took her a long time. . . . I was amazed she didn't give up. 'Take stuff one day a time,' she told me. 'Make things a little better one day at a time.' I still remember that." He pauses. "She didn't come round much, though, after my old man pulled a gun on her that one time out at the park."

There's a stunned silence in the car. My eyes go wide. Outside, the inlet's a flat gray blanket in the late autumn light.

"She didn't tell you that?" Harris laughs and shakes his head. "Man, don't your family talk about *nothing*?"

I blink and try to focus. Sitting beside me, Jesse starts drumming his hands lightly on his knees, almost like he's playing out a tune on the piano.

"Anyways, sorry again about the canoe. I won't do something like that again. But you know," his voice is more at ease now, "it sure was easy." Harris turns and looks directly at Dad. "You might want to do a better job of locking them up."

"Good idea," Dad says, smiling. "Thank you, Harris."

———

When we arrive, the parade is already underway, heading down Silverdale's main street to Waterfront Park where a stage has been set up for speeches and prizes. It's crowded and noisy with homemade floats, the high school marching band, and costumed walkers of every shape and size. We laugh about this year's most popular costume choice, the killer whale.

Everywhere, we see orca flags and banners, folks wearing orca headdresses, leaping orcas, orca fins, and—everyone's favorite—an orca pod, where every few minutes the marchers shoot sprays of water into the air. Someone hands Jesse a rubber orca nose mask, which he happily wears for the rest of the day.

Kings West Elementary School marches by with a set of posters showing L Pod's genealogy. SoundKeeper volunteers are here too, handing out their "Better Boater" guidelines.

"Holy crow, look there!" Harris shouts.

He points to a marching Mr. O'Connor, dressed as a mad scientist, complete with eyeballs dangling out of his sockets and an atom molecule on his cap.

"Man, that guy is craaa-zy!" Harris laughs, picking Jesse up and holding him high so he can see. As the last of the marchers pass, we tag onto the end and follow them down to the stage at the park, hungry now for lunch. The grass and picnic areas are packed. Occasionally, there's a burst of noise and shouting and we know someone has spotted the blows of real killer whales out on the inlet.

We're still hunting for an open space when I feel a tap on my shoulder.

"You came!" Lena smiles at me. I catch the look of surprise on her face when she sees Harris and Jesse, but there's no way to explain the whole canoe-hospital story now. "We got a table . . . c'mon." She leads us through the crowd to an area down near the embankment, near where a heavyset man sits, his back to the inlet.

"How are you, Larry?" Dad reaches out to shake Grace's father's hand. "Haven't seen you in a while."

I have . . . just last week. For a second, I consider asking how much money he's made so far from beach access, but decide against it.

"Is Grace here?" I ask Lena, looking around.

"Uh-huh. . . ." she nods. "We were out fishing together this morning. . . ."

I press my lips together but Lena knows what I'm thinking.

"What?" she asks, defensively. "I tried to call you to see if you wanted to come."

"Grace . . . *fishing?*"

"Marisa, listen," Lena whispers, brushing off the picnic bench and sitting down. "Her father took the whole family out on his big boat—you know, the *Cruiser*. She didn't have much choice, so she called me to come along." She laughs. "She stayed down in the cabin the entire time, even when we passed the pod, can you believe it?"

When Grace returns to the table, she acts at first like I'm not even there. Then I see her stare at Jesse, who has ketchup smeared all over his face.

"Oh, hello," she turns to me, smirking. "Babysitting today?"

Lena puts her hand on my arm. I let it go and focus on the talk at the table.

"These whales hang around much longer," Grace's father is saying between big bites of his salmon burger, "there won't be fishing left at all!"

Dad laughs uneasily. "I'm not sure we're at that point yet, Larry."

"No? We got a good run this year, but that pod was chowing down. I bet one of those buggers can eat . . . what, twenty-five, thirty fish a day?" He takes a long swig of beer. "And now we got *nineteen* of them out there."

Big surprise. Grace's father doesn't want to share the salmon with the whales.

"Larry . . . c'mon, it's chum. It's not like you're talking about kings," Dad says, naming the choice salmon species of the region.

I look around to see who else is listening, but it's only me, Grace, and Lena.

"I can only speak for myself, but I've got no interest in fishing for catfish or carp," Larry says. "I want the salmon."

"But salmon are *all* the orcas can eat," I say.

Larry looks up, surprised.

"Well, I don't know about that," he says, recovering quickly. "I've seen some gobble up seals lickety-split. Anyway, I'm getting tired of playing host." He takes another huge bite, and keeps on talking. "When I was a kid, we used to stand on the shore and pitch rocks at those whales if we saw them. Blackfish, we called 'em. Some people even used them for target practice." He shakes his head. "Can't do that today."

I stare at him, horrified. There's not much you can say to change the mind of a person who thinks like that. Still, I make a mental note to ask Naomi if what he said about the seals is actually true. I sneak a look at Grace, expecting to see a satisfied smile on her face. Instead, she looks mortified.

We're saved by a *tap-tap-tap* sound of a microphone. Everyone turns toward the stage where volunteers are busy setting up a table with prizes for the raffle.

A man steps up and addresses the crowd: "Folks, can I have your attention please."

He's wearing a bright yellow raincoat, even though there's no sign of rain. "Thank you. Wow! What a turnout this Halloween!" he says to a round of applause. "Welcome everyone. I'm Harold Langley, parade chairman. Before we bring out this year's costume contest winners, the Suquamish Tribe has asked me to make an announcement."

"Tribal representatives see this visit from the orcas as a powerful sign, and they're getting pretty worried. As much as we all love the whales, I think everyone agrees it's not natural for them to be here in the inlet. They're going to be keeping a close watch and they're planning a blessing ceremony, to fire up those orcas to head on home. They'll be letting us know the date on that soon. Okay now, time for some prizes!"

Mr. Langley continues talking, but his announcement gets me thinking. The Suquamish people have lived here at Sáq'ad, gathering food, hunting, and fishing for thousands of years. The orcas are a huge part of their stories and culture.

Harris turns to me and I can tell from the look on his face that we're both thinking the same thing. There's a good chance the Suquamish might know more about the ways of the orca than any whale researcher. If the Tribe is worried enough about the whales to schedule a blessing ceremony, maybe we should all start paying closer attention. Before it's too late.

CHAPTER 13

Orca Day 11

The alarm clock blares and I fumble to silence it, squinting in the dark. It's just past 4:00 A.M. Sunrise is still a good three hours away. Flopping back down in bed, I listen to the familiar sound of light rain, drumming on the houseboat roof. With a groan, I swing my legs over the side of my bed. Turning on the hot air blower as high as it will go, I dress quickly, shivering in the chilly air.

Last night, Dad announced that he'd offered to host a TV crew from the *Today Show* who were looking for a good location to film a segment about Kevin and the orcas. After checking with the houseboat management, he'd gotten the okay—good publicity, they said—and the early hour was set to broadcast the program live to the East Coast.

A horn beeps and I duck outside, shutting the door behind. In the foggy morning air, I can just barely see the dull orange and white of Kevin's van, parked up the road alongside the ramp. Pulling my jacket closer around me, I feel my way out to the end of the dock.

"The locals have been so cooperative," Kevin is telling the crew. "But the weekend boaters . . . let's just say I'm not sure out-oftowners are getting the message. We won't take lightly any activities that stress the whales."

I wander over to the dock edge and peer down into the water. It's pitch-black, and sloshes and gurgles, mixing with the creaking sounds of the wooden dock. As I walk back past the houseboat, the back door of the van swings open, flooding the road with light.

"Hello?" Naomi calls out. She crouches down and peers out, giving her eyes time to adjust to the darkness.

"It's just me, Marisa."

"What an ungodly hour to be up," she groans, hopping down from the van. "Whose bright idea was this? Too early even for whales . . . and too *cold*."

Together, we watch the crew set up to film Kevin out at the far end of the marina dock, where the view is the best. A light mist is falling. Over the inlet, a thick layer of fog lies low, blanketing the water. This has always been my favorite part of the day—the time when everything wakes up and the whole world seems new and fresh and anything seems possible.

After awhile, it gets boring; there's too much starting and stopping to check mechanical stuff. I can tell the TV crew were hoping they might get some shots of the whales, but there's no chance of that—not here, so close to the mouth of the channel.

Finally, Naomi gestures behind her to the glowing interior of the van. "Want to come inside? I have other stuff to do."

I nod and follow her, curious. I know Kevin's been using the van as his home away from home, sleeping down at the boat launch, but I'm totally not prepared for what's inside. The van's backseats have been removed and the whole space is jam-packed with equipment—a jumble of hydrophones, recorders, tapes, and a lot of other stuff I don't recognize. Plus there's all the usual things you'd need if you're basically living in a van—mounds of clothes, most of it pretty grungy, toothpaste, soap, a stray shoe or two, along with piles of journals, books, and magazines everywhere. I even spot a hammer and open box of nails. A rolled up sleeping bag is shoved into one corner, but I have no clue where Kevin would ever find a flat surface to use it.

"Pretty crazy, isn't it?" Naomi laughs, seeing me take it all in. She clears a space in one corner so we can sit. "He is *totally* obsessed . . . really. Whales are his whole life. Next time your mother tells you to clean your room, tell her about this place."

I blink, and try to think of something to say, but Naomi is already busy with something else. Two hydrophones lie on the floor at my feet—long black cords with a big bulge on one end. They remind me of the bull kelp that washes up all along Northwest beaches. I know what hydrophones do, but not really how they work. I pick one up and examine it, stretching it out to its full length.

"It's a simple thing, crude almost," Naomi explains. "The navy made them to listen for submarines. Easy to use, you just toss them over the side of the boat. But boy, what they let you hear is phenomenal." She turns and pulls some cassette tapes out from under a pile of socks. "Here . . . I made these near the shore by Chico Creek. Lots of activity out there. Seems whenever a pod is scattered around over a large area, something's usually up, like they're planning some kind of group effort. Want to listen?"

I take the headphones and place them over my ears. Naomi plugs in a second pair for herself, pops in yesterday's tape, and presses the "Play" button.

In an instant I'm transported into another time and place. Just like that day on the inlet when the whales surrounded our raft, my head, heart, and soul are filled with the sound of whale song. Except this time the effect is complete since the headphones block out any other sound.

At first, the short, sharp calls just sound like noise, but when I listen more closely I can tell there's more going on. One whale will make a sound and another will answer with the same or almost the same call. Sometimes the calls are soft and musical, something like *ow-ow-eeeee-ah-ah-ow-eeeee*. If you didn't know they were whales, you'd guess it was the call of a tiny bird—maybe a robin.

But other sounds are deep and growly, like they came from a totally different animal. Some sound like the whales are chomping or chewing, and still others—pops, clicks, and snaps—remind me of a machine or some of the electronic music Dad sometimes plays. Together, all the sounds blend, weave, and merge, creating a whole new audio world. The weirdest thing is, at times, it almost feels like I'm eavesdropping on a private conversation.

Naomi flicks off the recorder button and exhales deeply. "They get to me every time, no matter how often I hear them. Imagine hearing those sounds while sailing in the middle of an ocean on a boat with a wooden hull. Spooky. The early seamen thought they were the ghosts of drowned sailors." She turns the lights back up and the van floods with artificial light.

"Do different sounds mean different things?"

"Sort of, but we're not entirely sure. There are three types: clicks, whistles, and calls. We know for certain that the clicks are used for echolocation. You know what that is, right?" she asks, and I nod. "So when the orcas are tracking prey or navigating through narrow channels, or even checking out someone in a kayak, you'll hear the clicking sound."

"What about the whistles and calls?"

"Those are tricky. Calls are actually a series of clicks; we call them 'pulse trains.' Obviously, they're communicating *something*. We think there might be a difference of meaning depending on the tone, but that's just educated guessing."

Through the windows of the van, I can see the day lightening.

"The thing that makes this all so fascinating, of course, is that each pod, in fact sometimes, each sub-pod, has its own dialect, its own discrete set of specific clicks, whistles, and calls."

"What do you mean?"

Naomi leans toward me, her elbows on her knees. She clicks on the recorder again, and yesterday's recorded squawks and whistles fill the space of the van.

"L-25 sub-pod, the guys out there now, can recognize each other by their *own set of shared calls* that they learned as babies from their mothers. Think about that. One of the first whales captured and put on display in Seattle kept making the same calls in captivity as the rest of L Pod still swimming out in the wild. It's like every sub-pod has their own language."

Imagine—nobody can understand you, but you keep on talking. I think of Mom's letter that I threw away and feel a fresh pang of guilt.

Then I remember something important.

"Naomi?"

"Hmm?"

"That day, out near the Narrows, when the speedboat cut off the pod? Two whales pointed their tails straight up out of the water, then smacked them down on the surface. What does that mean?"

"Were there young ones around?"

I nod yes, pretty certain one of the calves was Muncher.

"That's called *lobtailing*," Naomi tells me. "It's pretty rare to see it since it's usually to warn off predators, and our Southern Resident orcas have such a benevolent relationship with humans.

But if the calves are threatened, by *anything*, and that day sure was a terror, the adults will lobtail."

Lobtailing. Seems like a good word to work into a conversation with Tal.

"Okay, ready for some more?" Naomi asks, handing me the headphones again.

I put them back on and suddenly an ear-splitting screech tears into my eardrums. I quickly rip them off, dropping them to the floor of the van.

"Sorry," Naomi says, looking sheepish, "I had the volume up high so you could hear details."

"What *was* that?"

"That, my dear, was the sound of an outboard motor cutting close by the hydrophone." She shakes her head and sighs. "Sound is amplified underwater. We don't hear half of what the whales hear."

That day at the Narrows, that motorboat cut off the whales—the memory flashes into my mind again—is that the kind of noise the pod heard underwater? No wonder they turned and fled the other way!

"So they *are* getting stressed. . . ." I say, imagining what that must be like trying to protect your calves from all the noise and chaos coming from a whole slew of obnoxious motorboats.

———

That night in bed, I can't relax. I pull out a book but keep having to reread the same paragraphs over and over until finally I give up. My mind is racing and I can't stop thinking about my conversation with Naomi. It makes me so sad. L Pod came to visit and we're behaving so badly. How can they possibly trust us not to hurt them?

And even though nobody is saying it outright, I'm convinced Kevin and Naomi are hiding the real truth—that each day the whales stay in the inlet, they're in more danger.

I turn off the light, still wide-awake. The motorboat noise is a clue, I'm sure of it, and I make a mental note to ask Kevin about it tomorrow. There must be a way to keep the boats away from the whales, give them a better chance to escape.

One thought keeps nagging at me, keeping my mind churning. Why didn't the pod leave back when the inlet was quiet, before all the boats came? Or at night when there's hardly any boat traffic? Does that mean there's another reason keeping them here, something more than chasing salmon or motorboat noise?

I'm tired of worrying over all these questions. I need to find some answers.

CHAPTER 14

Orca Day 13

On Monday when I arrive at Lions Field, the VW bus door is locked and Harris is outside waiting. He hasn't missed one chance to help with the whales ever since the canoe incident. Ten minutes later, Kevin finally slides the van door open and waves a silent hello, a phone to his ear. We climb in.

"Um-hmm. Yes, of course." As he talks, Kevin begins to sort photographs on a small makeshift wooden shelf rigged up against a wall of the van. "Absolutely, we'll be monitoring it closely." He motions for us to sit down. "Great. Okay, thanks for letting me know. Much appreciated."

"Well, *that* was interesting." He lays down the phone and turns toward us, looking like he could use a hot shower and a good night's sleep in a real bed. "State and tribal managers just agreed to cancel commercial fishing in the inlet starting tomorrow."

"Wow! That's good, right?" I ask, excited.

"Well, it's certainly unusual, but it does show some concern for the orcas," Kevin says. "What's not good is they've slashed their estimate of this year's chum run from 380,000 to 100,000. That's the smallest it's been in fifteen years." He shakes his head. "It doesn't leave a lot of wiggle room for commercial fishing and our hungry visitors."

"Couldn't they close the inlet to all marine traffic?" I ask.

"Yeah," Harris agrees. "That's a good idea! Why not?"

But Kevin is shaking his head. "Coast Guard rules make that almost impossible. It's considered 'an egregious breach of navigation rights.'"

Egregious. I'll have to look that one up to use on Tal, but I can already tell it can't be anything good.

"And we'd still have no guarantee that the whales would leave."

He reaches up to the top shelf and hits "Play" on the cassette tape player. More opera. This time the singer is Spanish or maybe Italian?

"We might be able to carve out a restricted area, to all but essential boat traffic, but that would be a last resort."

"But . . . isn't there a law to protect whales and other marine animals?" I ask, not ready to give up quite yet. "I remember my mom telling me about it. Wouldn't that make sense for what's happening here?"

"You're absolutely correct, Marisa, there is. It's the Marine Mammal Protection Act," Kevin nods. "But the act protects all marine animals, including whales, from being hunted or collected without a permit. What's happening here with boat harassment wouldn't apply."

Harris and I exchange a look. Every day now, we've signed on to help with anything Kevin and Naomi need done, but it still doesn't feel like we're doing enough. The rules make no sense to me, but Kevin has already moved on, so I drop it.

"Okay, I need y'all to sort these," he says, handing us each a big stack of photos. "I've marked the ID number of each on the back along with the date I snapped it. If you can organize them chronologically and by family, that would be awesome."

"What're these for?" Harris asks as we start to sift through the photos.

Most show dorsal fins or the upper surface of a whale, their blowholes, and a bit of their heads. Kevin plucks one back and lays it down on the shelf with the others, then flips it over. "L81" is scrawled in black marker on the back.

"Remember, I'm the fin-guy," Kevin says, crouching down and wiggling his fingers above his head again, just like the first time, and we have to laugh. "This one is Raina, male, about seven years old if memory serves me. I took this a couple of days ago. See the nick here in his dorsal fin? That tells us Raina had a run-in with a boat propeller. So all these photos are valuable, they give us clues: who the whales are, their health, all sorts of things."

He scans the shelf cluttered with photos. Watching him searching, I realize that the photos are laid out in the same configuration as my pod genealogy chart at home.

He points to an area in the upper left-hand corner. "Ah, here we go," he says, holding up a picture of a huge whale. "Almost all of Raina's family is in the inlet. His grandmother Baba, L26, is one of the oldest ladies of the group. She has three offspring. Rascal, Raina's mom who's in her twenties and Ballena, just a baby, maybe three or four." He taps his finger on another stack of photos. "Then there's Hugo, Rascal's brother, big guy, almost full-grown. He's gonna be our next sprouter," he tells us, sounding like a proud father. "By next season, his fin will be twice the size it is now."

Kevin shuffles through Rascal's pile of photos. "Now here's *another* photo, taken right after the group entered the inlet. See her blowholes . . . here?" He holds both pictures up side by side. "Not much difference, right?" He crouches down under one of the seats of the van, pulls out a drawer, and shuffles through its contents until he finds what he wants. "But . . . take a look at this." He shoves a worn looking photo into our hands.

Harris and I squint in the dim light of the van. The photo is a close-up shot, showing the upper surface of a whale, but the blow-hole looks different from the others—shrunken and shriveled, not taut and smooth like Rascal's. And the skin color—more gray than black, and mottled in places.

"Kinda creepy," Harris says under his breath.

"A couple of years ago, in '94, a bunch of whales got trapped in Barnes Lake up in Alaska," Kevin tells us. "Some never made it out; we had about three fatalities. What ya'll are looking at is a photo of one of the whales that died."

"See the difference here, the dull gray skin and the depression around the blowhole?" Kevin leans over and traces around an area with his finger. On the cassette tape a whole chorus of voices are singing together so furiously now it feels like the space of the van is almost too small to contain the sound. "On a whale, that condition is called 'peanut head' and it's the first sign of emaciation. Basically, those whales in Alaska starved to death. That's why we're taking all these photos of L Pod in the inlet, so we can catch the first signs of distress."

I study the pictures of Rascal, Hugo, and little Ballena.

"Ours are doing okay though, right?" I ask, turning to face Kevin.

"For now," he reassures me. "But animals that size . . . if they start to fail, it's hard to play catch-up. And we know the salmon won't last forever." He looks out the van window toward the inlet. "All the other plans we have in our back pocket to lead them out of the inlet are gonna be a whole lot more complicated . . . and controversial." He sighs. "So let's hope they take advantage of this week's good tide coming up."

I decide now is the time to ask Kevin the question that's been bothering me ever since Halloween.

"Are people blaming the whales for hurting the salmon run?"

Kevin quickly shakes his head.

"Low salmon runs are a bigger problem than Dyes Inlet. Still, 80 percent of the chum on this side of the peninsula run through Chico Creek. It's probably why the whales came in the first place. Slim pickin's elsewhere."

"What about seals?" I ask, remembering Grace's father's remark. "Would the whales eat seals instead?"

Kevin shakes his head. "Not on their menu. Transients will; those are the ones out in the open straits and the ocean . . . totally different animal. You wouldn't want to get anywhere near a transient in a kayak, not like you can with our sweet guys. I'll show y'all how to tell them apart sometime. Okay. . . . " he slaps his thighs. "Lesson over. Start sorting."

———

Now the only thing I want more than getting the whales home safely is to make sure Harris and Jesse get a chance to see them up close before they go. When I ask Harris if there's any way he and Jesse could meet me at the marina one day this week, early, before classes, he agrees in a heartbeat. The more time I spend with Harris, the more I've learned he can make things happen when he wants to.

We head out later that week, at seven o'clock, just as the sky is lightening. Sightings have been scarce these last few days—the whales seem to be pretty much going where they want to go, with no pattern—but I know from talking to Naomi where the most likely spots might be. I figure we have a window of an hour and a half to find them.

The water is glassy and calm, and the day windless as we row north out of the marina, and even though neither of us dares to say it, we're both aching to see the whales. We hug the western shore, and at times I catch myself holding my breath waiting for the whales' breath to come. But the water stays calm. Overhead, the crows *caw-caw* and the gulls *squawk* but the noisiest place of all is hidden. Without a hydrophone to drop overboard, the underwater calls of the orcas are lost.

Little waves lap on the hull. In the distance, I can hear the slow rumble of cars traveling on the eastern shoreline road. Even Jesse seems content to just sit, playing with the straps of his life jacket, dipping his hand in the water, or tapping out a little rhythm on the rowboat's hull.

The taps sound random at first, but when I really listen, something about the pattern starts to seem familiar. At first I can't place where I might have heard a sound like that.

Then I remember.

When Dad first taught me to kayak, he drilled it in that if I ever tipped over and couldn't right myself, I should tap on the hull in a specific rhythm. That way, he said, anyone hearing it would know someone was trapped underneath, and not think it was just abandoned. He taught me something sailors used, he said, to remember the long and short syllable pattern—seven beats—*shave-and-a-hair-cut-two-bits.*

And that's it! That's exactly what Jesse's tapping now on the rowboat's hull. *Shave-and-a-hair-cut-two-bits.* But . . . it must be just a coincidence. He'd have no way of knowing that trick, would he?

With orcas, you'll usually hear them before you see them— that *pfoosh* sound as they surface to breathe—but today it's quiet and the tapping lulls me. I so much want the orcas to come. But we don't have much longer before we have to turn and head back to the marina to make it in time for school.

I glance east toward the Tracyton shoreline, and notice five or six gulls diving at the surface. That could mean food scraps from orcas feeding nearby. I sit up straighter, trying to locate any sign of movement in the water.

The trick with spotting orcas is to not move your eyes too quickly from one place to the next, because they're constantly moving and by the time you refocus, they'll be gone. Mom taught me that. Stare at one spot for a minute, she said, then shift your gaze a little to the right and refocus. When it works, the whales should appear just slightly ahead of where you last looked.

Jesse's tapping continues. *Shave-and-a-hair-cut-two-bits.*

Then we hear it—the *pfoosh* of whale blows. Almost immediately, three whales surface near us, right off our port side. Two adults and a youngster. And there's no mistaking the rhythm of their blows.

The first gives one long blow—*shave.*

The little one follows . . . four short bursts—*and-a-hair-cut.*

Finally, the second adult answers . . . two distinct, extended blows—*two-bits.*

Jesse giggles and taps his message on our hull even louder. The whales repeat the sequence. I sit there stunned. It's like Jesse *called* them to come. And then the real show begins.

The little whale heaves himself up, laying his whole body across the head of one of the much larger whales, his mother? She tumbles him around and throws him off but as soon as he regains his balance he swims right back onto her head. And sure enough, she tumbles and throws him off again. They keep this up for several minutes. Off in the distance, I spot six or seven more whales playing with kelp, tail slapping, and spyhopping. Finally, after a good ten minutes, they all group up in the center of the inlet and swim southward, fast, toward the rocky shore.

I check my watch—it's time to go. A sad drizzle of rain is falling steadily now. As we row back to shore, I glance over at Harris.

"Did my mom ever say anything to you . . . about me?" He wrinkles his brow and holds my gaze. "You know," I shrug, "just anything she might've said about—"

Harris bursts out laughing, surprising me.

"What?" I whine.

"Marisa, you're kidding me, right? Your mom talked about you *all the time*. How hard you work, how much you love living here, how into whales you are. She told one kid how you liked cooking with your dad—I think she was trying to get him interested in eating something other than candy!" Harris says and we both laugh, Jesse joining in too.

"So, what about you and Jesse?" I ask, taking a chance. "I'm not trying to be nosy or anything, but you've had to do a lot for yourself, because of stuff at home, right? Are you doing okay?"

"Me? Yeah, it's cool, especially now that I'm older," Harris says. "It was kind of a love-hate thing with my folks, I guess. Pretty sure they loved me and Jes but they loved other stuff too, or maybe more." He drags his hand in the cold inlet water and laughs, but this time it isn't a fun laugh. "Things might've turned around if my mom hadn't died. At least that's what I tell myself. But she did die, right after Jesse was born with a whole slew of problems."

The water sloshes against the sides of our rowboat.

"That was the last straw, I think, for my old man. We bounced around in a bunch of foster homes . . . he'd always come home just enough to make sure nobody took his kids away for good. Lots of people helped, a little, but nobody helped enough to really make everything all right." He pauses. "Getting Jesse all the medical care he needs is the toughest," he says quietly.

We're at the dock now. A few other fishermen mill around, getting ready to head out. It's time to tie up and go.

"Maybe it's not for me to say, Marisa," Harris says, "but . . . somebody like your mom . . . there's gotta be a good reason why she left, you know? You're her *family.* She wouldn't just up and abandon family unless there was a damn good reason."

"I'm just afraid that—" I swallow. I haven't been able to explain my fear to anyone, not even myself. "I'm just afraid that maybe she'll decide she's not coming back."

Harris doesn't miss a beat. "No way. Never. Family was super-important to her, Marisa." He reaches across to ruffle Jesse's hair. "She told me once that no matter what, I needed to remember that Jesse and me were brothers. I needed to be responsible. I remember it real clear, 'He's *family,*' she said. 'Don't give him up or you'll always regret it.' A bunch of times, when things got rough, she told me to trust her." Harris looks at me. "Maybe you should, too."

And it takes all the effort I can muster not to burst into tears right then and there. After all that's happened these past weeks, a wave of real hope sweeps over me. I have the whales and Harris to thank for it.

———

That night, I sleep deeply and peacefully until—*CRASH!*

Water—the deafening sound of a massive wave slamming against my window jolts me awake. Stuff is flying everywhere. The houseboat is pitching and rolling with such tremendous force that I have to grip the side rails to keep from sliding to the floor.

"Daddy!" I scream out, then catch myself. "Hey, Dad!"

The table light smashes to the floor. Books slide off my dresser and land in a heap. I watch them fall like in a dream.

"Marisa!" I hear Dad's voice.

I manage to crawl out of bed but the houseboat is roiling so badly I can barely walk down the hallway. The door is open. Dad stumbles into the kitchen, stretching out his hand. I head toward him, clumsily making my way along, steadying myself with my arms against both of the walls. When I get close, I let one arm go and grab for his hand. He pulls me hard, up and over the main port door and outside onto the dock.

It's lighter outside, just barely dawn. Upland, the dark trees look strangely still—there's not even a breeze moving them. I stand there in my pajamas, bewildered, watching our houseboat rock wildly in its berth, hugging myself against the cold night air. The dock quickly fills with sleepy people pouring out of their boats.

"Those boats are coming in earlier and earlier. This is the second time we've been rocked this week!" says a man wrapped in a raincoat and wearing slippers. "Unbelievable!"

"It'll get worse," an elderly woman warns. "Just wait until the weekend."

A young woman sitting on the dock edge jiggles a crying baby. "Oh, please. I love the whales as much as anyone but . . . this is making me tired." She looks at me and sighs. I give her a sympathetic look as Dad rushes past, following a group of men toward the marina's maintenance shack.

"What happened?" I shout.

"Commercial tour boats. . . ." he answers. "Drove too fast through the Narrows. We got hit with their wakes. I have to help . . . the marina's water lines have pulled apart. I'll be back soon." I watch him hurry off and the conversation on the dock swirls around me.

"Idle in and idle out. That's all I ask. How hard is that?"

"Ha! Wishful thinking."

"How'd they like it if I drove a semi through their house?" asks the angry man in slippers.

I leave them to their grumbling and walk out along the length of the dock where there's a good view across the Narrows. Already, I can see damage to a few of the houseboat decks that have been swamped and banged around into their pilings. It's hard to think the movement of water could even damage water lines. But it's a narrow channel and those big boats have a deep "V" hull that pushes the water real hard, even when they're going slowly.

Across the water, lights are coming on at the yacht club marina at Phinney Bay, where Grace's father keeps his yacht. I stay there for a long time, thinking. As my eyes get accustomed to the dark, I can just barely see the vessels bobbing around, so I know the wakes have hit there as well.

By the time I walk back to our houseboat, the door is open and Dad is back, rooting around. The place is a mess. Things have been thrown down from every counter and table. Everything has fallen from the open kitchen shelves and furniture has slid and shifted, banging into the walls.

"Forgot my tools," he says, glancing at his watch. "Try to go back to sleep, it's still early. We'll deal with the mess later. Oh, and the water's off until they can repair the lines."

He finds his jacket under a pile of stuff in the hallway, gives me a quick kiss, and is gone.

"Bye," I whisper to the empty doorway. Sleep is the furthest thing from my mind right now. I pull out the broom and dustpan and start sweeping up pieces of broken dishes and glasses, wondering if there's anything else that can possibly go wrong.

CHAPTER 15

Orca Day 17

The damage from the massive wakes is all anyone talks about for days, and every story is worse than the last. The launching facilities at Evergreen Park and Lions Field have both been hit hard, and all up and down the inlet, stories pour in. Just this morning five people got tossed in the water when their sailboat overturned from the wake of a forty-foot yacht.

It gets so bad that the Coast Guard broadcasts a warning message on marine radio every hour, and sends out their cutter *Point Defiance* to enforce it. Worst of all, the big boats keep coming. With another weekend of whale watching looming, everyone is edgy.

After class, I duck into the bathroom. With the water off at the marina, I haven't showered in two days. One look in the mirror says it all. But Kevin's got a long list of stuff that needs to be done, so I give my face and neck a good scrub and have to settle for twisting my hair up into a double ponytail.

My newest job is posting "No Wake" notices along the shoreline. I head down the hill toward the inlet, a big stack stashed in my backpack. For close to an hour, I work my way south, stopping every 100 feet or so. As I tack the notices to the telephone poles, electricity running through the wires buzzes overhead. It's slowgoing, climbing off and on my bike, and the dirt kicked up from passing traffic on the road makes me feel even grimier.

Near Lions Field, I turn and head straight down to the shoreline, rounding the curve as the purple and white turrets of Tal and Bette's house come into view. Mut comes shuffling off the porch to greet me, followed by the familiar figure of Harris. As he comes closer, I can see he's carrying a small video camera.

"Wait, stop," he greets me, grinning. He holds up his hand. "Let me try this out." He brings the camera up to his face. "Move a little, maybe ride the bike back and forth."

Awkwardly I obey, making lazy figure eights on my bike. Mut pads after me as the camera whirs.

"Is that Tal's?"

Harris nods from behind the lens. "It's old, he says he never uses it anymore. I get to mess around with it now."

I glide my bike out of one final circle and come to a stop. It's only been a little over a week since Harris and Jesse have been at Tal and Bette's but it's like I'm looking at a whole new person.

"You look *great*," I say, without thinking, then quickly blush. "I mean, you look . . . better." I lay my bike and backpack down near the road.

"Yeah, it's cool. . . . " Harris nods, then laughs. "It's like being on vacation! These last couple years, I've been mostly trying to make sure Jesse and me get by, you know, eat okay and stuff. But man, I was losing steam. Now I'm kinda getting a plan," he says, his eyes shining. "Hey, did you know Bette's from Lummi Island? She's—"

"A plan?"

"Yeah," he shrugs, shuffling from one foot to the other on the sandy road. "I'm thinking it'd be good if me and Jesse spent more time with people—you know, people who can help." He slumps down against one of the big driftwood logs that separate the shoreline road from the beach. "I been in that house one week," Harris says. "*One week* Marisa, and I learned all sorts of stuff . . . about planes, cameras, fishing. Things I never even heard before. Man, those two have stories!"

I sit down beside him. The inlet is busy with boats, steaming back and forth.

With the toe of my sneaker, I dig a hole in the sand and fiddle with some dried-up seaweed. *Everybody needs someone to believe in them.* That's Mom—explaining the world to nine-year-old me. It occurs to me now that she probably shared similar advice with Harris.

"Has Tal started quizzing you on vocabulary words yet?" I ask Harris, but he just looks "flummoxed" which makes me grin.

"Hello!" Tal, calls out, walking down the porch steps. "To what do we owe this pleasant surprise?" Mut trots up to him, a long stick in his mouth.

"'No Wake' notices," I say, brushing the sand off my jeans. "We're posting them all around the inlet, and on the water on buoys, too." I pull a flyer out of my backpack and hand it to Tal. He takes the sheet of orange paper, pulls his reading glasses down from his forehead, and scans the page for a minute.

"'Boaters should be aware that they are legally responsible for any damage caused by their wakes,'" he reads aloud, then continues silently to himself. I watch as Harris wrestles the stick away from Mut, and throws it far down the length of the beach. But it's too far for old Mut and he watches it go.

"Hmm, well, in my experience," Tal says, "the only people who listen to these kinds of things are the people who don't need to. But I guess you do what you can do."

He hands the sheet back to me, and I stuff it into my pack, along with any gloomy feelings. Even if it's true what Tal said, he's someone who's taught me I have to keep trying.

"C'mon, I'll help," Harris says, so I haul my bike up to leave it on the porch and clip on Mut's leash. We plaster notices everywhere we possibly can, all along the length of the beach road, trekking uphill near the bridge, and then back along Tracyton Boulevard, hoping it might make a difference.

After almost an hour, at the cutoff to Lions Field we spot Grace, going in the opposite direction. For once she's alone, and she walks right by us—until she notices Mut.

"Hey, you have a dog?" she calls back.

Mut swivels around and makes a half jump toward her.

"No, Mut, down!" I yell.

"Mutt?" Grace laughs. "That's a weird name. Like mixed-dog mutt?"

"I hardly ever see you alone," Harris blurts out, changing the subject. "Usually you're walking with your crowd or your mother's driving you around."

I feel myself smile. It's kind of refreshing how Harris speaks his mind, doesn't waste time worrying about what people might be saying behind his back. I wait for Grace's reaction, but she surprises me.

"Not like usually, like always!" she laughs, straightening up. "I can't get my mother to leave me alone. I practically have to *hide* sometimes." She tips her head sideways and grins. "But today, Mom is out of town and Daddy is dealing with the trouble at the yacht club. So for once, *I-am-on-my-own.*"

Grace does a little spin right there on the road, then stops and looks at me. "Daddy says there was *thousands* of dollars of damage.

He was really worked up about it. But you probably know that. Don't you like, *live* on the water?" Before I can say anything, she notices the stack of paper sticking out of my backpack. "What are those?"

"Warning notices we're posting around the inlet."

"Give 'em to me," she says, her hand outstretched.

"Why?" I ask suspiciously.

"Just give them to me, okay." When I still don't hand them over, she rolls her eyes. "Sheesh, I'm not going to steal them or anything. I can put some up at the yacht club. Daddy will be so shocked that I even know about any of this."

Harris and I exchange a look, trying not to laugh.

"Sure, that'd be great." I reach into my bag and hand her the rest of the stack of notices. "Thanks." Smiling, she shoves them in her bag and heads home, not even bothering to read what they say.

———

On the way back, Harris invites me in to Tal and Bette's house. I accept, of course. It's Friday, so I don't have any homework I have to do just yet. Plus I've always wanted to see the inside of their crazy purple house. As you would expect from the outside, it's a hodge-podge mix of stuff inside as well. There are knickknacks and odd bits of junk everywhere. The kitchen, though, is filled with the heavenly scent of blueberry scones.

"Can you stay, Marisa?" Bette asks, wiping her hands on her apron. I see her take a good look at me. "My, you look a bit worn-out."

She's being polite. I must look like something Mut dragged up from the beach.

"That boy has been so good for Tal," she whispers, when Harris leaves the room. "He was spending far too much time thinking, if you know what I mean." Yep, I know perfectly what she means. "Now he seems to have a purpose again."

When I call to check in with Dad, he says the water is still off at the marina and Bette insists I use her shower. "Give me your dirty things, I've got a load of wash to do anyway," she orders, handing me two fluffy towels.

"Gotta look presentable for the crowds on Saturday," Harris jokes when he overhears. That gives Bette another idea. She glances at the wall clock in the kitchen.

"Harris is right. It's almost six already. You're just going to come right back here in the morning. Why don't you ask if you can stay the night? Harris and Jesse are in the basement bedrooms. You can stay upstairs in the tower. I think you'd enjoy that."

Dad says stay and I take what must be the longest shower of my life, feeling the hot water wash away three days of dirt and tiredness. When I'm done, Harris gives me the tour.

We wander around jam-packed rooms. One is filled entirely with tackle boxes, framed photos, and paintings of fish, plus half a dozen fishing poles lined up leaning against the walls. Another is Bette's quilting room. A whole room just for quilts. Two frames are set up and waiting with projects in progress and three gorgeous quilts hang on the wall, two Northwest landscapes and a third intricate design of flowers and hummingbirds.

When we make our way up the circular staircase to the tower room, I feel like a princess in a fairy tale, climbing up to her lookout. Harris pushes open the door and it creaks.

"You're not gonna believe this one," he smiles and we duck our heads to enter.

When I step inside, I catch my breath. Fancy windows with built-in cushioned seats encircle the whole room. Standing in the corner, near a daybed, an expensive-looking telescope points west. Through the windows, the inlet spreads out before us. Even in the fading light, I can see all the way south to the Warren Avenue Bridge and north to where the inlet dead-ends at Silverdale. Little specks of light, from the last few boats still moving on the water, flicker in the distance.

"Looks just like my view from the trailer park, don't you think?" Harris says and we laugh. It's nice to know we're good enough friends now that we can laugh about this.

When it gets too dark to see, Harris moves over to a small desk and clicks on the table light. It's a perfect desk, positioned to allow a half view of the inlet, with curved drawers running down both sides and little brass handles that make a satisfying little clinking sound when you touch them. I open and shut one drawer absentmindedly, thinking what it must be like to live here when I notice something glinting on the desk in the fading light. I lean closer to look.

It's a charm bracelet, lying on top of a thick stack of books.

"Oh!" I pick it up gently. It's really light and makes a pretty tinkling sound from the charms dangling off the chain.

"What's up?" Harris says, coming up behind me.

"It's a bracelet...look...."

I know right away it's not an expensive piece—the metal is a bright gold, too bright to be real—but I fall in love with it anyway. I examine each charm. There's a tiny American flag, a painter's palette with multicolored gems for all the different colors, a Christmas tree, a cat, an airplane, and a minuscule pair of baby shoes, each with an inscription on its sole: *Sept 4, 1975* on the left and the name *Carol Ann* on the right.

Plus one more.

"Look at the *orca*," I whisper, showing Harris the tiny leaping whale with faceted blue glass eyes. "I had a bracelet almost *exactly* like this, one that Mom and I put together. Every time we'd travel somewhere, we'd put a new charm on it. I loved that bracelet. I haven't seen it in years."

Harris is thumbing through the thick books where the bracelet was resting. "These are pretty cool," he says, handing me one with green binding and the words *Augustus 1990* embossed in gold. There are two more, same size but with different color bindings and different years.

I put the bracelet down and open the green book. Handwritten messages written in blue pen fill the endpaper and first page. Some have little hearts drawn next to the names, others "XOXO" in fancy curlicue letters. All the messages start the same way—*Dear Carol.*

"They're *yearbooks*," I tell Harris, lifting the bracelet again. "And this must be her bracelet."

"Who?"

"Carol Ann. The *Dear Carol* in the yearbooks. These are hers." A tingle runs through my body. "Have Tal and Bette ever mentioned a daughter?"

"Not to me," he says, still flipping through pages of past pictures of Augustus High School kids from years ago. *Swim Club. Forensic Society. Tennis Club.*

1975—the date on the baby shoes.

"Let me see something." I reach for the red yearbook Harris is holding, embossed with the date 1992, and flip the pages to the graduates' pictures in the back.

Parsons—Pawlak—Rizzo. Ragoza—Raimondo—Rea—Reese.

Silently, I pass the book to Harris. His eyes widen. One name stares up at us: *Carol Ann Reese.* Except where her picture should be, someone has taken scissors and carefully cut it away. All that's left is a gaping hole in the paper.

Carol Ann Reese is gone.

———

When I wake, it takes me a minute to remember where I am. The soft morning sunlight spreads its thin November rays over the water of the inlet, flooding the tower room with a soft light. Just as I imagined, the wall of windows offers a spectacular view.

I lie quietly, thinking about Carol Ann Reese. I thought about her all last night before falling asleep. What could have happened that was so awful Tal and Bette would never mention her?

From downstairs, the sounds of breakfast preparations float up. Bette has laid my freshly washed clothes out on one of the window seats. I dress slowly, then wander the tower room, almost in a trance. The telescope stands facing the window like a sentinel, and I run my hand along its length. It's not all that different from bird scopes or Dad's binoculars, and pretty soon I'm scanning the inlet like an expert.

Carefully, I move the scope left to right, repositioning the viewfinder. Boats of all kinds cluster in every cove and marina along the western and northern shore and I check for any big ones that might be entering the inlet. A ferry and one whale watcher steam in under the Manette Bridge, but the Warren Avenue approach is still clear.

Then, swiveling to the left, I see them—a cluster of black fins slicing through the water just north of the bridge. My knee-jerk reaction is to step back and of course the view disappears. I find the spot again, refocus, and hold the scope as still as I can. A small group of whales swims toward the mouth of the inlet, moving forward in a steady line.

Amazingly, there are no boats anywhere nearby.

From here in the tower, the whales seem a million miles away. I try to stay calm and count, 1-2-3-4-5 fins. Then I remember Kevin mentioning the beneficial tide. Maybe they're going for it! But— where's the rest of the pod?

The room is quiet except for the sound of the heavy mechanical clicking of the scope. Downstairs, I can hear Harris and Jesse moving around in the kitchen. I watch the group slowly approach the bridge—still forty or fifty feet away. I'm pressing the eyepiece against my socket so hard it starts to hurt, but I don't dare glance away.

"Harris!" I shout, keeping my eyes glued to the scope. "Come upstairs, quick! The whales are moving!"

Harris races up the stairs and together we take turns on the scope, watching as two of the largest orcas dive deeply, traveling under the bridge to surface on the other side with two spectacular blows. I hold my breath, but inside, I'm silently cheering. The rest are *so close* to the overpass now—probably only twenty feet away.

"Three to go," Harris says, stepping away from the scope so I can take a look. The largest whale in the group turns on his side. Then slowly and deliberately, I watch as he slaps the water once, twice, three times with his pec fin, almost like he's telling the others "Come on, follow me!" Then he dives. I track him with the scope, trying to anticipate where he'll surface, just the way Mom taught me. Two seconds later, up he comes on the other side, joining the two already there.

"He made it!" I shout. "But . . . "

I watch as the three orcas begin circle swimming in a holding pattern.

"What?"

"They're not leaving." I turn to Harris. "I think they're waiting for the little ones to follow."

We wait, watching. A few long seconds pass. "Maybe we oughta call Mr. O or Kevin," Harris says finally, fidgeting. "Let them know some, at least, made it out."

I bite my lip. "Is Tal downstairs?"

Harris shakes his head. "He's helping Kevin get patrol boats out. Bette's out with Mut."

Maybe he's right. Kevin could make sure Rich Passage is clear for the pod to head out to the Sound. I check the two smaller whales again. Nothing. They're still in the inlet, swimming around like they have nothing better to do than play. C'mon. Follow your pod!

I check again for the three who've already passed under the bridge.

"Wait . . . where did they go?"

I scan everywhere, swinging the scope back and forth wildly. Are they underwater? Did they move out to the open Sound that quickly? Even in my panic I know this isn't the sensible way. But I can't help it, I feel this desperate need to find them.

"See anything?" Harris asks, moving quickly behind me.

Yeah, I do, but I can't believe it.

"They're coming back!" I watch as the three orcas slowly pass back under the Warren Avenue Bridge and reenter Dyes Inlet. "They got out, and now they've come back."

CHAPTER 16

Orca Day 18

Harris and I keep watching through the scope, checking to see if maybe the whales will reverse their course again and head back out, but they don't. Finally, we give up. In the space of fifteen minutes, the mood in the tower has gone from ecstatic to gloomy.

Why did they come back to an inlet with almost no salmon, after finally finding safe passage out?

I sink down on the edge of the daybed. On the desk, Carol Ann's yearbook still lies open where I left it yesterday. The questions, to so many things, keep piling up.

"What could have happened?" I say, thinking out loud. "Why would someone cut her picture out like that?"

"Lots," Harris laughs roughly. "Which bad story do you want to hear?"

His answer startles me. Still, even after all of Mom and Harris's stories, I don't really acknowledge how hard growing up is for some kids—and how lucky I am.

"You know, they sat me down the other day, Tal and Bette," Harris tells me. "Wondered if maybe Jes and me would think about staying here permanent."

I look up at him, surprised, but he shakes his head.

"Makes sense now, knowing they had a kid who left. But I can't do it. Can't see how I can abandon my old man."

"But . . . after all the stories you told me? Why? He's never been there for you, or Jesse." But even hearing myself say this, it feels wrong.

"He's my old man," Harris shrugs. "I can't just leave him 'cause he made some stupid choices." He hesitates, just a heartbeat. "Don't get me wrong, I'm mad at him for lots of stuff. But he always comes back." Harris laughs. "Kinda like these crazy whales! If I just walk away . . . I figure that doesn't make me much better than him."

"Hello?"

Footsteps on the stairs, then Bette pokes her head in the room. When she sees the look on our faces, she shifts into nurse mode. "What's happened? Is everything all right?"

We tell Bette about the whales' abandoned exit, and she relaxes, just a little. I'm used to this from Mom—each crisis put into perspective. Then I see Bette notice the yearbooks.

Abruptly, she walks across the room and starts rubbing my back, like she's known me forever, like she's *my* mother. I stand there frozen, trying to decide if I should ask her to stop or move away, not knowing what I really want.

"I remember when she was born," she says, out of the blue. "I was so happy to have a little girl." Her hand drops from my back and she smiles sadly. "She didn't stay little for long, though." When she looks at me, I have the weird feeling she's seeing someone else.

"I came upstairs to check on you this morning," Bette explains, "just to be sure you were warm enough, it gets so cold up here in the winter."

The beautiful silver wolf pendant that calmed me that night at Evanston Memorial still hangs from Bette's neck, catching the first rays of the sun. And I remember Harris telling me Bette was from Lummi Island. Listening to her now—the rise and fall of her voice—I wonder how it didn't occur to me earlier that she might be Native American.

"Why keep all her stuff lying around?" Harris blurts out. I give him a quick look, but Bette's face is calm.

"I can't seem to put it away." She starts rubbing my back again, like it was a magic lamp that could conjure up Carol Ann Reese back from wherever she was. "I thought I'd better tell you her story before you asked Tal. He still can't talk about it very easily."

"Who cut it out?" Harris asks.

"She did," Bette says, turning toward the windows.

Her words hang in the air.

"Why?" I whisper. "What happened?"

"I wish I had a good answer for you, Marisa," Bette says with a sigh. "We've been asking ourselves that question since she ran away. We were both working fifty-hour weeks. She was troubled. We realized too late. There were many reasons, I suppose."

Bette walks slowly over to the huge window. I can't see her face. I know I should stop asking questions but I can't. For some reason I *need* to know.

"Where did she go?"

"We spent the better part of two years trying to track her down. We only heard from her once. She'd had a child . . . at eighteen. She sent a letter, saying she was doing fine. . . ." Bette pauses, staring out at the expansive view of the inlet. "She asked us not to try to find her."

I have to ask.

"Did you stop looking?"

Bette shakes her head. "We couldn't. We wanted so much to hold her again, know she was safe, tell her. . . ."

Bette stops and turns to face me.

"With everything your mother's going through now . . . all the old feelings have come rushing back to me. She was our *child*. We had to do everything in our power to find her, even though in the end, all we're left with is hoping and believing that one day when she's ready, she'll be back."

I'm imagining what it's like to be Carol Ann Reese and leave home at sixteen or seventeen and not see your parents again. Or to grow up like Jesse, without knowing your real mother at all, when it hits me what Bette's just said.

I stare at her, wide-eyed.

Bette realizes she's let a secret slip. "Hon, your mother only confided a little bit to me about her plans. She was there for me when we lost Carol Ann and so I tried to help her now. Honestly, considering her work, I think she was surprised by her own reaction," Bette explains, but I'm only more confused.

Seeing my face, Bette gives me a little smile, but it fades quickly. "Don't be upset sweetheart . . . I shouldn't have said anything."

I feel the weight of the bed shift as Bette sits down next to me.

"Your mother's very private. She didn't tell me much about what happened . . . before . . . in California. But she felt like she'd been given a second chance and needed to take it."

The air in the room feels heavy, like in a dream when you try to run or swim but your limbs will only move in slow motion. My head keeps telling me to *do something*, but my body doesn't obey. Maybe that's a good thing, because suddenly I feel out of control, afraid I'll do something stupid like push them both out of the way. I close my eyes and try to think.

"C'mon," Bette reaches out and pats my hand. "Your dad

just called. The water and power are back on at the marina. Let's get you home."

There's a sharp pain in my chest. I stand and follow Bette numbly out of the room, not turning to look back at Harris.

Bette knows where Mom is and why she left . . . and I don't.

———

The water is cold and it's dark. Salmon swirl all around me as I swim with the pod, matching their pace. Leaping and diving together, we form one enormous group moving forward. I'm one of them but at the same time, I'm me.

The others don't seem worried but I know I need to surface soon and breathe, but I can't. We just keep going, swimming, diving deeper in the murky water. The only sound is a muffled gurgling, the background music of the underwater world.

Suddenly, a strong current pulls me away from the group. Roiling water swamps me. Something massive is passing alongside. I try to turn and see what it is, but my body doesn't obey. A second ago, I was gliding swiftly along, now I can't move an inch in any direction. I'm trapped, surrounded by circling whales. I'm not afraid. Their huge flukes move up and down just inches away. When their bodies rise, I can see their underbellies. There are little ones, too. They tumble and roll with their mothers. I seem to have feet now, I can feel myself treading water, watching the whales play all around me. One approaches me sideways, so close, staring at me with its deep eye.

Then something goes very wrong. The pod maneuvers into a huddle position, the calves in the center. Their great bodies begin to heave and together, they send out a sound like nothing I've ever heard. The largest whales begin, and one by one the others join in until the whole pod is speaking together with one voice. Agitated labored breathing . . . a great hruumping that seems to rise up from the very depths of the sea.

I can't hold my breath any longer. I desperately need air, but can't move. A ringing begins, becoming louder and louder until the sound fills my ears. A low rumble adds to the noise, and as the pressure builds, the rumble seems to grow, and grow, and grow until the sound itself is pressing down on me, squeezing what little air is left out of my protected space.

I try to push myself up and out of the water to reach the fresh air. All around me the whales continue to hruump, hruump, and now they too, are desperate for air. But none of us can rise to the surface. Something huge and dark is holding us down. The ringing won't stop. Something invisible and strong is holding us down . . . under the water . . . under the surface. I hear crying all around me. I'm crying too—if we don't surface soon, we'll all drown!

I bolt upright in my bed, terrified. My chest is heaving. The phone won't stop ringing. I lie back, forcing myself to breathe in and out, trying to calm my racing heart. The hands on my bedside clock say 6:00 AM.

In a cold sweat, I stumble through the dark hallway, into the kitchen. Dad is just hanging up the phone. My dream is quickly fading, but it's shaken me. The rumble . . . that wide, black shadow— I can still see it hovering over me and the pod, its shape vaguely familiar somehow. . . .

"That was Tal," Dad says. "Sunday morning and there's a line for boats already."

I nod dully, my mind still in my dream. The whales were in trouble, deep trouble, but they weren't alone. Whatever was above them was keeping them from rising up to breathe. . . .

Climbing onto the stool, I hug my knees to my chest, pulling my nightgown down over my legs.

"I sure could use your help today," Dad sighs. He sits down

next to me, and rubs at his eyes. "Honestly, I don't know how much longer we can keep this up."

I don't think Dad means the whales, but he might as well.

———

The drive to Mud Bay is painfully slow. I fidget in my seat and Dad keeps glancing my way. As we cross the Warren Avenue Bridge, I crane my neck toward the inlet. Every possible kind of craft is visible on the water—the big whale watchers, yachts, rowboats, kayaks, powerboats, Jet Skis—all of them jockeying for a good viewing spot. If the whales are out there, there's no way to know.

Mud Bay is a madhouse. At least fifty people are lined up and waiting for Dad to open so for the next hour, I help as much as I can. Together we get people signed up and outfitted with gear, but I'm distracted and keep making mistakes.

By one o'clock, we're done—there's nothing left to rent.

I pace, up and down the dock. I tidy equipment and clean out the life jacket bins. But I can't seem to shake the emotion from this morning's dream—the scenes keep running through my head. I need to see the whales, make sure they're okay.

"Dad?"

He's sitting and resting outside, on one of the waiting area benches.

"Hmm?"

"There's not a lot to do until the boats start coming back."

He laughs, sprinkling a sugar packet into his hot tea. "Is that a problem?"

"I was just wondering . . . do you think maybe I could leave for a little bit?" I sit down beside him. "I won't be long, I promise. I just want to see if everything's okay."

Dad is quiet a second, then suddenly he stands up. "Okay . . .

let's go." He flips over the "Closed" sign hanging from a hook above the door, then pulls the door shut and locks it.

I stare at him. "What are you doing?"

"Well, like you said, everything's all rented. No sense staying here. Let's both check on the whales." He turns around and smiles.

"That's what you really meant, right?"

I swallow. Do parents always know what you're thinking?

"But what if somebody wants to tie up early?" This isn't like Dad to do something spontaneous and against the posted rules.

"They can wait." He sees the shock in my face and laughs. "Don't look at me like that! No one will be back until at least four o'clock. C'mon." He reaches out to pull me up from the dock. "This was *your* idea, remember?"

———

The bridge is crowded. We're almost halfway across when we hear it—the shrill call of a long, low siren carrying over the inlet. I quickly roll down the window.

"Is that Kevin?" Dad asks, trying to drive and look at the same time.

"I don't know!" I shout over the noise of traffic. It's impossible to get a clear view from the bridge deck, but the warning being broadcast across the inlet is unmistakable. I think I see a flash of a yellow flag but we're driving east. My view of the inlet is pretty much blocked.

Dad and I exchange a worried look. Without a word, he presses down on the gas pedal and our car accelerates. Ten minutes later, I'm racing down to the SoundKeeper tables at Lions Field.

I spot Naomi and Lena near the dock launch and struggle through the crowd toward them. "What's going on?" I mouth wordlessly to Lena but she just shakes her head. Naomi is on her radio, talking and pacing. The crowd swirls around us.

Waiting, I take my first good look out across the inlet. A gray cloud of pollution from the boats' exhausts hangs over everything. So many vessels are packed together, I can't even see the water in some places.

"Guys, this is a real problem," Naomi says, turning to us. She blows her bangs out of her eyes with a puff of air. "I need your help. One of you come with me; the other stay here." She shoves a walkie-talkie at Lena. "I've got Kevin on an open line. Make sure you don't lose him. This button will connect to my pager. Call *immediately* if Kevin needs me."

She shows Lena how to switch channels, grabs a granola bar from the table, and rushes toward the dock. "Marisa, follow me!" she calls back.

Lena looks terrified. She's holding Naomi's walkie-talkie as if she'd just been handed a baby with a poopy diaper. I offer up a smile, then hurry off after Naomi, wondering what's in store for me.

———

"They're grouped up over by Chico Bay," Naomi explains when I catch up. "From what Kevin says, it sounds like they've abandoned their normal feeding behavior." She chucks her gear in the eighteen-foot inflatable, and reaches out to help me climb in.

"That's bad, isn't it?"

She nods. "Whales won't cluster in a tight defensive group like that unless they're pretty stressed. Big surprise. . . ." she scoffs, starting up the raft's engine. "Look around!"

We motor out and see clearly now that the entire inlet is jammed with boats. They're everywhere, stretching across the full width of the inlet and as far north and south as the eye can see. In some places, you could literally walk across the water by stepping from boat to boat.

"How many do you think there are?" I ask, stunned.

"We've counted close to five hundred."

I think I must have heard her wrong. "Five hundred boats? *Here?* In the inlet?"

She nods and slows the engine to maneuver the raft around a clump of kayakers. Five hundred is such a huge number that it loses all meaning to me. I try to imagine being one of the whales now, fighting for space in a 100-foot-deep inlet, but the image it conjures up is too terrible.

"But, isn't there some rule? Some kind of limit on how many boats can get in?"

Naomi snorts. "Right. Try restricting the right of navigation and see what happens," she says, echoing Kevin's answer that day when I asked about closing the inlet to boat traffic. "It's like asking people to give up their guns."

We continue a slow tour of the inlet, following a wide, flattened circle pattern from south to north. The air stinks with the smell of half-burned fuel. In some places, I see the rainbow shine of oil gleaming on the water. My head is spinning.

"What can we do?"

"We need to get them to back off, scatter them as much as we can. . . ." To our left a speeding motorboat cuts us off, "and get 'em to SLOW DOWN!" Naomi shouts as their passing wake rocks us. She picks up the bullhorn lying on the bottom of the raft.

"WATCH YOUR WAKE!" she calls out.

The offending boaters turn at the sound of the warning. One waves sheepishly but the boat doesn't slow down.

Naomi sighs. "We have no legal authority. There's no state or federal law controlling the speed of boats in the Narrows or Dyes Inlet. Nobody's even been given *one ticket*." She reaches into her bag for a clipboard and tosses it across to me. "From now on, keep track."

Her pager beeps. She checks it, then punches some buttons on her walkie-talkie. Kevin's voice comes over the line, scratchy but urgent.

"Where?" Naomi shouts. "Okay, got it." She clicks off the radio. Her face has lost all color. "Hang on," she says, pushing the raft's measly engine as hard as it will go. We speed off toward the western shore, near Chico Bay, moving through relatively open water now. I don't understand where everyone went, until up ahead I see a huge cluster of boats jammed together, with more speeding toward them from all directions. Naomi slows the engine.

"Marisa, can you drive this?"

Our raft? I hesitate a second, then nod. "I think so."

"Forward to speed up, straight up for neutral, backward for reverse. Got it?" She doesn't wait for an answer. We change positions and I take hold of the controls. Naomi moves to the edge of the raft and switches on the megaphone.

"BOATERS, TURN OFF YOUR ENGINES. ALLOW THE WHALES ROOM TO MOVE. REPEAT, PLEASE TURN OFF YOUR ENGINES."

With all the motors running, you can hardly hear her even with the megaphone. She repeats the message. Once. Twice. A third time. I try my best to keep the raft moving steadily forward. Easy enough. Hands on the throttle and shifter. No problem. I've done this before.

Still, I'm sweating in the cold inlet. The current feels more muscular than I thought it would. I concentrate so hard my head starts to hurt.

The tangle of boats seems to grow with every 100 yards I navigate. As we reach the crush of boats, I have to jockey for space with whizzing racers and 2,000 horsepower yachts. We're almost near the center of the vortex now. Sometimes, a space will open up and I see the flash of black and white or a plume of mist rising up from the water's surface.

There are way too many vessels for us to corral them. Whenever we manage to scatter a few, others come up and take their place. The whales are close by but this is all wrong—terribly wrong. The boats have the pod encircled with nowhere for them to go.

It's last night's dream. Come alive, right in front of my eyes.

"Turn off your engine and back off!" Naomi screams at two guys in a racer no more than six feet away.

"Will you just shut up and let us experience this?" one of them yells back, making a rude gesture. Unfazed, Naomi repeats the warning. They ignore her and make a sharp about-face in their boat, sending a plume of exhaust fumes directly in our faces.

"NEVER, in two years with SoundKeeper, have I had to bullhorn boats to back off and have NOBODY pay any attention. Damn it!" she explodes. "They're pushing the whales up against the shore!"

She's furious and I have no clue how to help. Frightened, I grip the controls even tighter. I can clearly see the backs of the whales humped and clustered at the surface—there's no way they would dive under, not with all those hulls underneath the water. My mind is racing, imagining various outcomes to this mess—all of them bad. Then, off in the distance, two spots of yellow catch my eye. SoundKeeper vessels! Like beacons of hope, they flicker in the murky smog-filled air over the tops of the boat hulls.

"Naomi, look!" I point awkwardly with my chin in their direction, reluctant to release my death grip on the raft's controls. Naomi grabs for her radio. When I hear the familiar crackle of Kevin's voice, I allow myself a tiny glimmer of relief, listening to them coordinate a plan.

"Marisa, drive us forward," Naomi instructs, clicking off the radio. "We're going to give this one last shot." She gives me a weak grin. "Let's hope they don't know we're bluffing."

I drive our inflatable directly at the wall of boats, half a dozen times. Naomi orders all engines off, and threatens citations for noncompliance. Kevin's raft, approaching from the north, does the same, even though we have no authority to follow through. Tal handles the southeast edge, and in the SoundKeeper vessel beside him—video camera running—is Harris.

After fifteen wild minutes of maneuvering, we've managed to punch out a good-sized opening. Once some of the engine noise is cut, I hear the whales again.

Hruump. Hruump. Hruuuuuump.

In a rush of water and fins, they regroup, diving to escape north toward Silverdale, one or two boats still racing after them. As they swim off, I count ten animals. A couple yards out, they start up their rhythmic breathing: twenty seconds down, blow; twenty seconds down, another blow. After three or four cycles, they hump their backs together and dive deep.

Pfoosh—Pfoosh

"They'll stay down now for about seven minutes, then probably surface again farther away," Naomi says, as we stare at the empty surface of the water. She gives a short laugh. "Amazing they don't just cut and run as fast as they can."

But they're not all gone. A small whale breaks the pattern, surfacing nearby.

"That's gotta be a kid," Naomi says. "You gotta love the little ones who can't hold their breath too long."

The little orca pops up once, twice, enjoying his private little water spot to frolic and play. When he arches his back and dives, I spot his saddle patch. It *is* Muncher. Now I'm positive. I shiver, wishing I'd had time to bring along some gloves. Muncher spyhops again. This time he stares straight at me with his perfect round eye and a chill runs down my spine. He holds my gaze for a long minute, does one last dive, and is gone.

"Be careful," I whisper. "Just hang on a little longer. We're going to help you get home. I promise."

As the water settles, Grace's dad's words come back to me about the times he would pitch rocks at the whales when he was a kid. Nothing's changed, really. The whales are still at risk, except now we're shooting them with cameras instead of guns.

CHAPTER 17

Orca Day 19

After the chaos of yesterday's herding, everyone's mood darkens. The Suquamish Tribe moves up the day for their blessing ceremony, and everyone is grateful. Right now, the whales can use all the help they can get.

A light rain is falling as Lena and I row north from Mud Bay toward Rocky Point. Everything is silvery gray, one of those Northwest days when it seems as if the whole world has no color. The ceremony is set for noon but things are still quiet. We secure our rowboat, an old aluminum one that Dad let me borrow, and wander the dock, waiting for Harris and Jesse to show up.

Pretty soon folks start arriving. Some paddlers tie up at the dock in canoes, rowboats, or kayaks. Others who'd been gathering up on the grass, near the picnic shelters, start moving nearer to the dock. All the jostling for a good viewing space reminds me of that day on the bridge deck when the boaters turned back the whales. Kevin said when people think they only have one chance to see a whale, they'll act irrational—do anything to make sure they don't miss out—even if it could mean hurting the very creature they've come to see.

"That's missing the bigger picture," he told us, frustrated. "People need to look at the consequences of their actions. Everything is connected."

One chance. Mom and Bette both talked about getting a second chance. But a second chance to do what? It's been so crazy I haven't had time to check for any letters at the post office, but I resolve to ride by again first thing tomorrow.

"How are the new digs?" I hear Lena ask.

"Jesse loves it," Harris says, ruffling Jesse's hair. He's wearing a new hooded sweatshirt and squeaky clean sneakers. "I'm not as used to . . . you know, always having people *around*." He shrugs. "But it's not forever."

"They officially counted 550 boats on the inlet yesterday," Lena reports, reading from the newspaper she's spread out on the grass. "Not including people watching from shore—"

"I overheard one lady say she came all the way from Florida!" Harris interrupts. He sits fiddling with his video camera, rewinding and viewing the footage he shot yesterday on the inlet.

"They're calling an emergency meeting at the Sons of Norway Community Lodge," Lena reads, "to see if they can bring charges against any of the boaters. Apparently, it's a federal crime to harass marine mammals. Who knew *that*?" She looks up, and I wave my hand, smiling. "Oh, right, of course," she says and we laugh.

"Well, I got it all here if they wanna see it," Harris says, patting the camera. "It's not pretty."

"C'noos!" Jesse yells, jumping up and down. He pulls on Harris's shirt, pointing toward the open inlet. "Harris, lots of c'noos!"

In the colorless light, I can just see a thin line of dugout canoes approaching the marina, their hulls each carved from a single cedar log. Some are painted black, others white, each with graceful curved half-spiral tops, and prows carved and painted with Coast Salish designs.

"There's *so many*," Lena says, climbing up onto one of the dock railings, trying to get a better view with her binoculars. "Looks like fifty or sixty canoes."

"They can't all be Suquamish," I say. "They must be from other tribes."

"Yeah, I think you're right," Lena confirms. "The carvings are all different." She lowers the binoculars. "Wow," she says softly.

The line of canoes slowly emerges from the gray landscape, the paddlers pulling together. As more and more canoes become visible, they seem to fill the entire inlet spread out before us.

Then we hear it—drums and chanting voices. It begins softly at first, but rises in intensity. The sound wafts toward us in the thin air. I close my eyes, wishing I knew what the words mean, but maybe it doesn't matter. Just like Kevin's opera music, just like the whales' songs, I feel the way I did when Naomi clicked on the recorded tapes. The voices of the paddlers are all moving together, breathing together, singing together, as if they're one being.

What was it Kevin said? *People miss the big picture. Everything is connected.*

"Maybe they're out there, waiting to answer," Harris whispers. "Maybe they'll really come."

I catch his eye and we both smile. Listening, I can almost convince myself that the whales really do understand the song. It is meant for them after all, isn't it? Maybe they feel the connections, too.

Yes, please come and let us bless you. Come and let us help you find your way home, even if we can't get rid of all the speedboats, and cars, and people—

"Look, they're circling!" Lena announces.

As the first canoes approach the marina they peel off, the paddlers circling one to the left, the next to the right, until they form two semicircles, opening up a direct line for half a dozen of the larger canoes to dock. It looks so cooperative, just like the synchronized swimming of the whales.

Some paddlers are wearing the traditional conical cedar bark woven hat of the Coast Salish. Some have woolen blankets, pitch-black with swirling red spiral and oval shapes, covering their shoulders. A handful wear their own versions of ceremonial clothing, some making due with just a red shirt and a headband of woven rattan. One woman's hair is decorated with white yarn braided with red beads. One paddler simply covered his ears with a woolen headband—the kind you'd wear when you're skiing.

The smaller canoes rest in a holding pattern now, facing the dock. We watch as paddlers from many of the Coast Salish tribes—Suquamish, Swinomish, Samish and Lummi, S'Kallam, Tsartlip, Chehalis, Quinault, and Puyallup—pull their canoes side by side, traveling together for the blessing ceremony.

The drumming stops and words in Lushootseed, the language of the Southern Salish, echo over the water. I think about what they must mean. I know a few words in Lushootseed—*Sáq'ad* is "Dyes Inlet" and *qál'qaləx̌ič* means "killer whale." I think I'm hearing both of those words repeated now, but I can't be sure.

I've gone to a few programs that the Suquamish Tribe offered. One year I even pulled in a canoe on a special paddle journey up near Lummi Island. I know how important traditions and values are to their culture. Some Coast Salish tribes even consider the orcas to be their ancestors. They see a connection, too, between all living things on the planet. I'm not sure I really understood what that all meant until right now.

As their words wash over me, suddenly everything becomes crystal clear.

The Suquamish are right. Kevin is right. Everything *is* connected, from the fish to the forests to the oceans. From Harris and Jesse and their dad, to me and Mom and Muncher and all the visiting orcas. I keep trying to make sense of everything that's been happening, but I've been going about it the wrong way—looking at all the pieces of the puzzle separately. The clues are here, but I've been chasing them at the surface, like the orcas do sometimes when they fish. Instead, I should be following the whales' example when they dive deep. I need to look closer, look deeper, below what I see on the surface.

We watch quietly for close to an hour, until the ceremony ends. As the tribal canoes start to separate, I take our rowboat out past the dock, adding my own prayer for the whales, sending them the wisdom and strength to find their way home. Mom always says there are no coincidences. I know the Suquamish Nation held their blessing ceremony to help the orcas find their way home, but maybe being here has helped me find my way, too.

I pull hard against the water, moving us forward against the incoming tide, repeating my prayer for the whales and hoping it's powerful enough to bring Mom home, too.

CHAPTER 18

Orca Day 20

On Monday morning, I bike over to the post office so early I have to wait for Charlie to arrive and open up. It seems to take forever by the time he unlocks all the doors, turns on the lights, and checks whatever else needs checking. Finally, he gives me a little nod and I scoot in.

It's been over a week since I've stopped by and there's a lot to sort through. Quickly, I spread everything out on the counter, separating the junk mail from the bills and magazines, looking for a simple white envelope with blue handwriting.

Nothing. How can that be? She said she'd write, even when we talked on the phone that day, but nothing has come since that one letter that I stupidly tossed weeks ago.

I start over, going through every piece in all the piles again, and by the time I'm done a sick, sinking feeling has worked its way up through my body. Mom *knew* I wasn't reading her letters. What if she decided to give up? There'd be only one person to blame. Me.

"Oh, and there's this too," Charlie says. "Probably missed the forwarding period."

He hands me a blue greeting card envelope, hand addressed to

"Abigail Gage" at our old East Sixteenth Street address. Stamped across the front in black ink are the words "Undeliverable." There's no return address, but the original postmark reads REDLANDS, CA.

——

All day, the letter to Mom rests in my backpack. I should just give it to Dad, but what I really want to do is open it. That would be wrong, I know. It's Mom's letter, not mine, but the idea keeps tick-tocking back and forth inside my head. I can't stop thinking about it and I sit, restless, through my classes. Whoever sent Mom this letter is with her now, somewhere in California, I'm sure of it. It's the "important person" she needed to meet.

And inside is the reason why she left.

By the end of the day, I've convinced myself that opening and reading the letter is okay. It's been in the post office so long already, whatever it says inside is probably old by now, not important, but . . . maybe I should just check to be sure . . . right?

Right.

——

Tonight, before the emergency meeting at the Sons of Norway, while Dad's getting ready, I quietly close the door to my room and sit cross-legged on my bed, holding the little envelope. I turn it over in my hands, squeeze it, hold it up to the light.

Finally, I shut my eyes and rip it open quick, like pulling a Band-Aid off a nasty cut. From inside, I extract what feels like one thin sheet of paper.

Slowly, I unfold it, lift it to my face, and open my eyes.

Dear Mrs. Gage,

After mailing you my first letter, I panicked. I'm guessing you've received it by now and are probably still in shock that the son you gave up for adoption years ago has contacted you. With all my heart, I hope that you decide to contact me at the phone number I provided. But if you cannot or do not want to ever meet me in person, there are a few things I don't want to leave unsaid.

Because telling you my name and phone number isn't the same as sharing with you a little of what my life has been like.

So here goes...

The words get blurry because my eyes are filled with tears. There's more, a lot more, but I stop reading and fold the letter up clumsily, shoving it back into the envelope. I don't even bother to look at the bottom to see the name of the writer. It doesn't matter. What flashes through my mind are Mom's words to Harris about taking care of Jesse. *Don't give him up or you'll always regret it.*

I lean back on my bed and stay that way for a long time, as the room darkens and night comes to the inlet, until finally Dad calls my name and it's time to go.

————

The Sons of Norway Lodge is packed. Just about anybody who has some kind of business on the water is here. Dad and I slip into two of the last open chairs in the back, just as the meeting is getting under way. There are familiar faces everywhere. I spot Kevin and Naomi up at the front, talking to a man wearing an official-looking uniform.

Dad notices me looking. "He's with the Coast Guard," he whispers, leaning over.

The lights in the room dim. The projector clicks through image after image showing Saturday's herding. The pictures are grainy and blurred but what they show is unmistakable. Two rows ahead, Harris turns and points to the flashing pictures. I shake my head, not understanding. When he grins and taps his chest, I realize he's telling me those are *his* pictures.

Kevin steps up to the microphone and the room quiets.

"Folks," he addresses the crowd, unsmiling, "what we witnessed this weekend was Penn Cove without the net."

Chairs scrape and people cough nervously. I scan the room to see if I'm the only one who doesn't understand. "Whatever strategy y'all had completely fell apart," Kevin says, turning to the officials from the National Marine Fisheries Service. "You allowed the whales to be harassed, corralled, and captured with 500 vessels. SoundKeeper will *not* allow this to continue."

He talks for twenty minutes, challenging the different agencies to come up with a plan to manage the number of boats in Dyes Inlet. When he's finished, he asks if anyone has questions or comments, and dozens of hands shoot into the air.

Everyone wants to have their say. Some get so agitated they just shout out without waiting to be recognized.

"Just ticket 'em!" one man yells. "What kind of enforcement have you got if you ain't gonna ticket?"

When I turn to look, I'm shocked to see that the speaker is Grace's father.

"Close the inlet!" others call. Harris turns to me, grinning.

Listening, I lose track of what everyone wants and why they think they should get it. Finally, a Port Washington official takes the microphone and tries to settle everyone down. There's a final call for questions and Dad surprises me by raising his hand.

"Not a question," he says, standing up, "an announcement. Mud Bay Kayak is cancelling all commercial kayak outings on weekends and holidays, starting tomorrow—" a few people clap encouragement, "as long as the whales remain in the inlet."

A reporter from the *Inlet News* is busy scribbling in his notepad. This is huge.

"And what's more," Dad raises his voice, "I challenge all commercial whale watching operators to do the same." He sits down to a loud round of applause.

"Can you *do* that?" I lean over and whisper, scared but excited and proud at the same time.

"I just did," he whispers back, "and with Tal's blessing, too." He reaches over and squeezes my hand and I squeeze back.

———

After the meeting, we regroup for pizza at Garlic Jim's, and the first thing I ask Kevin is what he meant by "Penn Cove without the net." But Bette answers instead.

"It was terrible, just terrible," she says, shutting her eyes against the memory. "Anyone who was there and witnessed it will tell you that."

"It was in 1970. August, I believe," Tal says. "Not too far from here, up at Penn Cove on Whidbey Island." He glances at Bette. "We spent summers there at the time, so we were around a lot, exploring."

I shake my head, still not understanding.

"The whales make a long trek at the end of summer," Kevin explains. "They meet up with other communities north of here at Possession Sound. We know now that they do this annually, but years ago there wasn't a whole lot of understanding of how whale societies were structured." He slides three pizza slices onto his plate. "All folks knew was that sometime in late summer, there was a good chance of finding large groups of traveling whales, sometimes numbering over a hundred."

"That's all they *needed* to know," Tal says.

"How's the pizza?" Lena asks, arriving with Grace. No one answers.

"They sent out speedboats to set off small explosives," Tal continues. "It disoriented the whole pod pretty quickly. Then they used backup boats and small aircraft to herd them into Penn Cove. It's a small inlet, easy enough to section off a corral with nets going down on all four sides."

"Those whales move *fast!*" Harris exclaims. "How'd they manage it?"

"Oh, the orcas led them on a pretty wild chase, you can be sure of that," Tal says. "The adults split up, trying to lure the hunters away from the calves. But the boats were relentless."

"Who *were* these people?" Lena asks. She's still standing, holding her plate of pizza.

"If you're asking about the people who did the actual work," Tal tells Lena, "I think they hired from the local community."

"You see, back then, you could get a permit to capture whales," Kevin explains. "But I don't think we'll ever really know where the big money came from to finance these operations. You have to remember . . . there was a *huge* demand from aquariums for whales back then."

"It was the young ones they wanted especially," Bette whispers.

Everyone's food is sitting untouched, getting cold. I think about Bette and Tal's lost daughter, Carol Ann. And I think about Mom, and the letter from her son, resting now in my jacket pocket, and I suddenly know, without any doubt, that all the questions I have must be only a fraction of the ones Bette and Mom have wondered and worried about all these years.

"Did it work?" I ask.

"Unfortunately it did, Marisa," Tal sighs. "But not easily and maybe not in the way they intended. They managed to corral eighty whales in the pen that day."

"Eighty?" Grace says, her voice thin.

"Man, I thought you were gonna say something like eight or ten!" Harris says. "But *eighty*?"

"They kept them in that pen for days and days," Bette says. "You could hear their screams for miles. I remember walking by early one morning. . . ." She pauses and gives Tal a quick look. "With our daughter, Carol Ann. She was four or five at the time and she was terribly upset. She kept asking, *Why are they crying, Mommy? Why are the whales crying?* It just broke my heart."

I feel a lump steadily rising in my throat. When I look over at Naomi, tears are streaming down her face.

"Bette reaches for Tal's hand and holds it in her lap, stroking it. "From that moment on, we became ardent environmentalists, didn't we, hon?"

"But . . . why didn't people do something?" Grace asks. "Didn't anybody try to stop them?"

I expect Tal or Kevin to answer, but it's Dad.

"People thought about going out at night and trying to cut them free," he says. "Some might've tried, I don't know. You have to understand, they had men on boats with rifles out there guarding them day and night."

Was he there? Was Mom? What would I have done if it'd been me? Would I have fought for the whales, taken a stand, or just stood by and waited for someone else to act? I feel my face redden, remembering that I have Lena to thank now for helping our whales.

"How did it end?" Lena asks.

"Not well," Dad says. "They separated the adults from the calves, and of course the mothers were desperate to reach them."

"Anybody tried to take Jesse, I'd do the same," Harris says, looping his free arm around Jesse's shoulder. His forehead is wrinkled up in a scowl. And it dawns on me how, just like with the whales, so many feelings, so many connections exist below and beyond what's easy to see on the surface. You have to chase them to find out the truth. Unless you do, no one has the right to judge.

"One mother and four youngsters drowned trying to charge the nets," Kevin says. "Of course, they tried to cover it up. . . ." Tal tells us. "They hired men to go out in the middle of the night and dispose of the whales that drowned."

"It wasn't pretty," Bette answers.

"What did they do?" I have to ask.

"Slit them open and filled them with rocks, then put anchors on their tails to sink them," Kevin says, his voice flat.

The tears start and I close my eyes against the horrible image Kevin's words have put into our minds.

"There was a huge public outcry a couple of months later when the bodies washed up on shore. It made national headlines," Dad says. He looks at me. "I've always thought it was part of why your mother moved up here from California . . . she got pretty involved with organizing local protests."

That made perfect sense . . . why Mom loved the whales so much. But why have I never heard this story before?

"Penn Cove was key to passing Washington State's ban on orca captures," Kevin says, glancing at me. "And a few years later to the Marine Mammal Protection Act. Probably the only good things that came out of it."

"But people forget," Tal says, answering the question I didn't ask, "they harvested six youngsters in the end." I cringe at his choice of words. "Yes, Marisa, that's the word they used: *harvest*. Awful, isn't it? Funny thing . . . once they got them and pulled up the net to release the others, they wouldn't leave. They went right over to the beach and just milled around there . . . for the longest time." He clears his throat. "Anyway, a call went out to aquariums around the world. A few stayed in the US but the rest were sent to other countries: Japan, France, Australia. None lived for very long really, except one: a six-year-old female that went to Miami."

"She's been there for twenty-seven years now," Kevin says and I hear the anger in his voice. "A four-ton orca swimming around in a tank the size of a backyard pool."

"I went there once to see her. . . ." Naomi says. "They gave her a new name . . . Lolita." She swipes at her eyes with a tomato sauce–stained napkin. "She still makes the same calls that L Pod uses . . . after all those years."

I close my eyes and see a blur of tangled images: baby whales, struggling mothers, armed men guarding the pen. I imagine Bette and Carol Ann walking by the cove in the dark night, listening to their cries. I can't imagine what it would be like to lose or leave your child—or give one up—for whatever reason, but I've learned a new truth. *It happens all the time.*

I shove my hands deep in my jacket pockets. My fingers close around the letter from my half brother. I understand now why he needed to write to the mother he'd lost. And why Mom needed to leave to find him again.

CHAPTER 19

Orca Day 21: Veterans Day

Okay, if we can't close the inlet to boats, and we can't get the boats off the water, we'll have to lure them out," I announce to Harris, Lena, and Grace. With no school today, we spend the whole morning brainstorming ideas to present to Kevin and Naomi on how to get the whales out of the inlet.

"How's that different from herding?" Harris asks.

"It's *totally* different," I say, but I'm already thinking of other ideas. "Or we could dump fish and hope they follow. Or—"

"You'd need a lot of fish," Lena says and I frown, because she's right.

"You have a better idea?" Harris asks, but not in a mean way.

"Hey!" Lena says, after a long pause. "What about using some kind of *music?*"

"Ha!" Harris laughs. "That opera Kevin's always playing sounds an awful lot like whale calls!"

"That's true," I tap the pencil against my cheek. "But Naomi said they tried that up in Alaska. The whales wouldn't follow."

Nobody has anything else to suggest, and I shake my head in frustration. Not a one of these ideas is going to impress Kevin.

We need something we can prove will work.

I think for a minute, remembering watching the whales through the telescope in Carol Ann Reese's room, seeing the three orcas return because the calves didn't follow. What did Tal say once? *Orcas are careful not to stay and forage in any one area for too long.* He was talking about overfishing and the effects on the environment, but thinking about his words now gives me an important clue.

I push my chair back from the table and stand up.

"We're thinking about all this the wrong way!" Everyone stares at me, waiting. "The whales aren't staying in the inlet because they *want* to. They're staying because they *can't* get out on their own."

I haven't said anything new, not really, so why does it feel new to me? "Before we can figure out how, we need to figure out why."

Lena sighs, breaking the silence. "Sounds good, Marisa. Let's just figure it out quick, okay? Before something really awful happens."

————

The images of the Penn Cove capture keep replaying in my head. I can't sleep and toss and turn for what seems like hours. Finally, I give up and click on the light. I have no idea what time it is but it doesn't matter. Lena is right. We have to figure out why the whales won't leave before it's too late. Inside my head, a familiar voice starts up again.

People need more than just dreams. They need action.

It's Mom, of course, with her practical–idealistic "I-can-change-the-world" approach. Oh, how I wish she were here to help me now. She would absolutely know what to do. But at least one thing is clear to me—it's time to stop worrying and take action. Right now.

Getting out of bed, I dress quickly. It's cold and the irony of what I'm struggling with hits me. All this time I've spent trying to figure out why my mother left and now I'm trying even harder to figure out why the whales won't leave.

I have no new plan, but I need time. Time to think. Time by myself out on the inlet, where it's quiet. I guess I'm like Mom that way. She used to take long walks alone if she needed to work out a problem. I go to the inlet. Tossing a few things into my backpack, I scribble a quick note to Dad, leaving it on the kitchen counter where he's sure to see it. Stepping outside, I shut the door as quietly as I can and bike slowly up the embankment to Veneta Street. The sky is still dark—there's at least another hour till sunrise.

As I coast down the hill to Mud Bay, there's just the slightest hint of light in the sky and a soft drizzle falls on my face and hands. It's the second week of November and the unusually dry fall we've had won't last much longer. Soon the winter rains will start. Not that the whales will care, but it might make a difference for the crowds.

For once, I find myself wishing for the dry season to end.

I tuck my bike under the dry eave of the storage shed and drag out our old kayak that Dad keeps here in storage. Slipping on a life jacket, I climb in. As soon as I start paddling, the sound of pulling water soothes me. All I want to do is drift and think, so I head west, toward the widest part of the inlet.

But in the fifteen minutes it takes me to reach the center, the rain stops and a thick layer of fog rolls in from the south. Dyes Inlet is like a bowl. Once a storm front or fog bank moves in, it sinks down to cover the inlet until an even stronger weather front blows it away or the sun burns it off. Mom and Dad talked about it constantly— always being prepared for unpredictable weather.

I feel my nerves rising. Okay, nothing to worry about really. How far off course can I go? It's a pretty small inlet, except . . . it's not really. My muscles tense, making each new paddle stroke harder than the last.

The memory of Harris and Jesse struggling in the water comes back to haunt me. Even a small inlet is huge when you're in a kayak in the dark and no one can see you. My little boat is alone, with no whale watchers out here now. But somewhere under the cold water, there's a pod of nineteen killer whales swimming around. I shiver. I know perfectly well that orcas are fish eaters, but I also know they're curious. A single kayaker out on a foggy inlet might attract that curiosity.

But there's no sign of whales anywhere. Even if there were, I'd never know it because everything is blanketed now in fog so thick I can barely see the front end of the kayak. I look left, right, ahead. The color is totally drained from the landscape and I paddle on in a silvery world.

I grit my teeth and concentrate, trying to remember everything Dad ever taught me about kayaking in bad weather. Part of me goes into automatic mode, calling on the instructions he drilled into me so often in our time spent on the water. Slowly, I maneuver the craft so I'm facing the direction the wind is blowing, then raise my paddle and push it down vertically, into the water as hard as I can, to stop the kayak from drifting.

Then I wait.

It's impossible to estimate how far I've already gone from the shore. Dad says staying in one place is better than blindly rowing yourself into the path of another vessel.

Use your ears, Marisa. Listen and reposition yourself if you need to.

I listen.

At first, all I think I hear is the sound of my own blood pulsing in my ears, but when I concentrate I know there's something more. A low but steady rumble seems to sink right down into my bones. Every few seconds, I think I see a flash of red, but I can't be sure if I'm just imagining it.

The rumbling gets louder—it's almost a roar now. I'm drifting . . . I can feel it. . . .

I try as hard as I can to wrap my mind around what could be happening, when—

WWwwwwaaaaaaaaaaaahhhhhh

My free hand shoots up to cover my ear. The kayak wobbles and I nearly lose my grip on my paddle. Breathing hard, I squint up and stare. Whatever sky I could see before is blotted out now—looming over me instead is a gloomy, black shadow. It feels oppressive—like it could crush me at any moment, push me down deep into the water, where there's no air—

No air? Wait! This has happened before, this massive black shadow . . . this sense of foreboding. . . . I've lived this before in my nightmare!

Then, suddenly, everything clicks and I know *exactly* where I am . . . directly under the Warren Avenue Bridge.

Time slows to a crawl. I sit there in the fog, paralyzed, gripping the vertical paddle, afraid to let the kayak drift even a foot in any direction. The Warren Avenue Bridge spans the inlet's exit to Rich Passage. If I cross under the bridge and get caught in the Passage's current, I'll run the risk of being pulled out toward the open water of the channel. And in this fog, my chances of getting myself reoriented and back into the inlet will be slim.

I take a few deep breaths, trying to decide what to do next. But the next minute, my concentration is broken again, this time by a different sound—*pfoosh, pfoosh, pfoosh*—the unmistakable exhalation of a whale blow mixed with the sound of gurgling water.

I swivel left, then right, trying to gauge how close they might be.

Suddenly, a whale spyhops on the port side of my kayak—close enough for me to clearly see him even in the thick fog. I gasp and he slips silently back under the water. His mother comes next. She's four times as large, and spyhops so far out of the water I'm afraid my little kayak will capsize. I struggle to keep level, imagining the headline in tomorrow's paper: "Kayaker Mauled by Salmon-Starved Whales."

Again the two whales appear together, but this time they don't spyhop. Instead, they surface not more than twenty feet off my starboard side and start echolocating me like crazy. I've still got my paddle stuck straight down in the water, trying to steady myself in the current, and I can feel the *rat-tat-tat* pulses directed my way.

My heart thumps in my chest, but even through my fear, I can't help but marvel at their beauty. The little one—it's Muncher again, I'm sure of it—stays nearby, floating, the closest he's ever gotten to me. His skin is as smooth as a beach ball. He stares right at me, his little eye patch focused, while his mother makes a big blow, then does a deep dive.

Mom's entire body seems to be crosshatched with scratches and scars. I can clearly see nicks and cuts on her dorsal fin. She's magnificent all the same. Seeing her saddle patch so closely, I'm amazed that what looks like pure white from a distance is really more like mottled gray, with subtle variations.

Then something under the water bumps the end of my sunken blade, hard, throwing me off balance. I grip the shaft of my paddle with both hands, my knuckles white with fear, but the paddle swivels sideways anyway as the kayak starts rocking back and forth wildly. For a panicked second, I'm certain the whale is going to push my kayak up from below the surface of the water. Or knock me over. But seconds more pass and nothing happens.

Then, *plunk*, it bumps my paddle again. The mother whale surfaces maybe a hundred yards away, behind me to my left. Muncher does a quick little dive and sprints off in her direction. Reunited, they spyhop, dive, and circle lazily at the surface, ignoring me.

All behavior is communication.

My breath comes in quick little bursts. Could it be . . . are they waiting for me to follow? In a heartbeat, I decide to trust them.

I scramble to reposition my paddle, keeping my eyes glued on my two rescuers, my hands numb from the cold. Somehow, I manage to angle the blade into the water and execute a 180-degree turn. Oriented, I begin paddling toward the circling whales.

When I'm as near as I dare, Muncher spyhops and gives out a little squeal. His mother dives again. I pause, scanning the water, waiting to see where she'll resurface. Muncher and I both locate her at the same time. He quickly races toward her. I follow.

We continue this pattern for two or three more cycles. Slowly, I relax into paddling again, my fear mostly gone now. It becomes a game and quickly we make distance. Only once does Muncher become distracted when he spots a cache of salmon shoaled up in some shallow water and spends a few minutes chasing at the surface.

Finally, his mother calls him back with her *rat-tat-tat* call. The second he leaves, four seagulls swoop down to scavenge the spot. That means there are still salmon, and I make a mental note to tell Kevin.

The fog has lifted slightly now and when I peer toward the shoreline edge I can just make out a few spots of orange and blue— the brightly colored kayaks of Mud Bay. Thirty feet from the dock, Muncher and his mother begin their slow circling of my kayak again.

Each does a deep dive under me, coming up on the inlet side. They roll on their sides, moving together in perfect unison. Two pec fins—one big, one little—reach toward the sky in a salute, then come down to slap the surface. Fountains of water and mist spew through their blowholes. One last time, they dive together and disappear.

Alone again, I breathe in the cool, salty air, pulling my eyes away from the rippling surface of the water, reluctant to end our play. But in my heart, I know it wasn't a game. The fog has all burned off now. Shallow water sloshes around the kayak. I sit motionless, not yet ready to reenter the world.

In the distance, the Warren Avenue Bridge rumbles on, its load of cars and trucks getting louder and louder by the minute as morning traffic picks up. I stop and really listen and the constant noise snakes itself into my head. I can feel it taking over my body, slowly but surely erasing the images and sounds of the whales.

And that's when I make the connection. That's when I know, without a doubt, what's stopping the whales from leaving the inlet.

CHAPTER 20

Everything is crystal clear now and I know exactly what I need to do. Hauling my kayak out of the water as quickly as I can, I drag it back up the dock, dumping it near the storage shed and throwing my life jacket down. Then I'm on my bike, racing back across the bridge and north on the still-deserted roads toward the Tracyton boat launch. Only one car comes toward me, its headlights blinding bright.

I have to find Kevin. I know he'll understand.

I make the two-mile ride in record time, skidding down the gravel embankment and running right up to the van. I knock hard on the back door. No answer. I knock again, louder this time. I even jiggle the handle but it's locked.

The dock is empty. The air is still chilly but the sun has broken through the clouds. I have no idea what time it is but don't care. I decide to wait. Kevin and Naomi will be working even on a holiday.

Five minutes later they both come walking down the ramp, carrying steaming cups of coffee.

"Marisa? Hey . . . you okay?" Naomi asks when she's closer. I'm soaking wet and must look half wild.

"I was out on the water and the whales came!" I burst out, breathless. "They came in the fog . . . it was Muncher!"

"Whoa! Slow down. . . ." Kevin puts up his hand. He quickly unlocks the van and they guide me inside, where it's warm. "*Where* were you?"

"The inlet. I was out on the inlet and—"

"What in blazes were you doing out there *alone* in the fog?" Kevin yells. "Marisa! This isn't a joke. I don't think I can—"

"No!" I cut him off. "I'm fine, really. But I figured it out! It's not what we thought . . . it's not the vessel traffic on the water. It's the *bridge!*" I tell them, barely able to contain my excitement. "It's all the noise from the traffic on the bridge that's blocking the whales from leaving!"

I watch as Naomi sets a pot of water on the camp stove and wait for Kevin to announce how brilliant I am and how everything will be all right now. But his expression doesn't change. He slides a tape into his cassette player and flicks a switch. The music, quiet this time, fills the cramped compartment. Then he turns toward me, his face as stern as stone.

"How do you know this, Marisa?"

The quiet in his voice unnerves me.

"I . . . I was right underneath the overpass. It's huge and dark, and it casts this awful shadow on the water. . . ." I pause, searching for the right words, trying to explain that feeling of dread that filled my whole body as I drifted under the roadway.

"Here you go, sweetie." Naomi hands me some hot tea.

"I think that's why they won't go underneath it." I take the cup from her, grateful. "And this isn't the first time . . . it happened once before, and I saw it! The time you thought they might leave when the tide was good, remember? The mothers went under the bridge but they came back because the calves wouldn't follow!"

Kevin sighs loudly, running both hands through his hair.

"I really appreciate everything ya'll have been doing to help the whales out here," he says. "It's a tremendous job of stewardship—"

"There's a shadow, too, when they're under it. . . ." I continue, remembering my dream of swimming with the whales, nearly drowning under the massive blackness looming above me. "The calves *always* stop when they get near the bridge, and won't cross below it. And the mothers won't go without the calves. So none of them leave."

"We'll get them out. We're working hard on all sorts of ideas," Kevin says, and I can hear the impatience in his voice. "Everything from attracting them with recorded whale calls to pushing them with a flotilla of boats—"

"None of that will work," I cut him off. "It won't make any difference. They'll just get to the bridge and stop. We have to do something about the *bridge!*"

"Such as?" Naomi asks.

"I . . . I don't know," I mumble, taken aback by her direct question. "I guess I thought you'd figure that out."

Everything I know about whales I learned from Mom. After hearing the Penn Cove story, I realize why she loved them so much. I breathe and try to reach out to her, channel her.

"Marisa, the whales entered the inlet under the bridge," I hear Kevin say. "Have y'all considered that? Why would they have trouble leaving the same way?"

"Because they came in at night, when it was *quiet*," I whisper, almost to myself. "Now . . . every time they try to leave, the noise turns them away."

There's a tapping on the van door. Harris and Lena poke their heads inside, and my heart does a little flip, I'm so glad to see them.

They do a quick read of the situation and stop dead in their tracks.

Naomi looks back and forth between us.

"Kev, it is true that the pod doesn't usually travel at night, " she says, her voice tentative. "Chasing salmon was probably what brought them in and broke their pattern, but we all agreed that was unusual."

"Yeah!" Harris chimes in. "And now the salmon are gone, so there's nothing to chase the other way to attract them out."

"That makes sense," Lena nods.

"Well," Kevin says, his voice now tense, "I'm glad all the *experts* are in agreement, but even if I was convinced, how exactly do you propose we do this? I can't even get the port to restrict vessel traffic. I think history shows our priorities when it comes to humans versus whales."

Suddenly, I can tell that Kevin is angry at himself, not at me. He's frustrated that he hasn't been able to help the whales. He works so hard and cares so much about them. Why has it taken me so long to notice that?

I think back to the day Lena and I first spotted the whales. Was there anything I was forgetting? Food and fear are the only things I can think of that would keep the pod here for three weeks . . . it's why they came now, and why they came over forty years ago, that time that Mr. O'Connor told us about, when he was just a "wee tyke."

Forty years ago is 1957. . . .

My mind is racing, and something else flashes in my brain, something Tal told me—that day I first met him and Mut outside his purple house. Things were different when he first moved here, he told me. What year was that? Later than 1957, I'm sure of it. . . .

My head hurts from thinking so hard. Kevin's opera music is

blaring now—this time the singing is in some language I can't even identify. What chance do I have to convince two scientists—with no hard evidence—what I know in my heart to be true?

I take a deep breath, and force myself not to look away. "There's only one thing we can do that will help the whales," I announce. "We have to close the bridge."

———

It seems so obvious to me now. Of course. Close the bridge and the whales will leave. The solution has been staring me in the face for days, waiting for me to see it. I try to read Kevin and Naomi's expressions but their faces are blank.

"Do you *really* think we could finagle a permit to close the bridge?" Kevin asks.

I glance at Naomi and neither of us dares say a word. Kevin's eyes grow wide when it dawns on him that this is *exactly* what we're asking.

"Y'all have got to be kidding me," he says softly. "That's the one primary commuter bridge that connects the east and west peninsula, and I'm supposed to ask people to drive clear around the inlet—all the way to Silverdale—while we wait for the whales to take their sweet time deciding to go home?"

All the way around the inlet . . . when Tal moved here, he had to drive *all the way around the inlet* to go from the east to the west peninsula. . . .

That's it!

"I have proof!" I jump up, screaming over the opera singer, and nearly knocking over my teacup. "When the whales came into the inlet the last time, forty years ago, *there was no bridge!* That's why they left. That's why they didn't get stuck here before. The Warren Avenue Bridge wasn't built until 1962!"

There's a stunned silence.

"How do you know these things, Marisa?" Naomi asks grinning.

I grin back, thrilled to have found the last missing piece, and I make a silent promise to thank Tal for his "Facts of the Day."

"All we would need is *one night*," I say, and—"

"One night? We don't know for sure they'd leave in one night. No," Kevin says in a firm voice. He looks at me sharply. "I've got very little time left and no resources to waste. I've got to choose the most viable way to get these whales out of this inlet before things get ugly. I don't have time for an untested idea. The whales are starting to avoid the boats . . . pacing, like caged animals."

I feel myself go white, listening.

"Kev, we've seen them approach the bridge almost thirty times," Naomi says, giving it one more shot. "Maybe we could try—"

"No, enough!" Kevin snaps, cutting her off. "Thank you, but enough," he says, struggling to soften his voice. "If you really want to help, there's a city council hearing scheduled on Saturday to discuss wakes. If we can win that one, it's gonna help the whales by slowing down traffic. Marisa, maybe you could—"

But I've stopped listening. My shoulders tighten and a hot anger rises inside me.

They're pacing like caged animals.

Kevin's a scientist. How can he ignore the evidence? Numbly, I push my way out from the tight group and start to run. I'm suddenly back in that place where I swore I wouldn't go. The words of the woman at the Whale Museum in Friday Harbor echo in my head—*You take good care of Muncher, okay?*

I run because I'm afraid. I run because a choice Mom made long ago still haunts her and I'm afraid if I don't help the whales now, I'll be haunted too.

CHAPTER 21

Orca Day 24

For two whole days, it pours down rain. Not the usual Northwest drizzle you can ignore, but honest-to-goodness downpours that put everyone in a bad mood. The only good thing is it keeps boats off the water. The whales scatter themselves around the inlet too, keeping everyone guessing where they'll pop up next.

I go into avoidance mode, letting other people figure out what to do next. On Thursday morning, I convince Dad to let me skip school. I need time to think about the whales and school's not the place to do it.

"I just feel achy," I call out through the bathroom door, "maybe it's the flu or something. . . ." Finally, it works.

After Dad leaves, I sit at the kitchen counter and think through my options. I can forget everything and go on with life the way it was before the whales came. I can follow the rules, doing whatever Kevin and Naomi need, and go to meeting after meeting, where it'll be all talk and no action. It doesn't feel right. I can't abandon the whales now, not after working so hard. But I don't know how to help anymore.

By noon, I'm pacing around like the whales, navigating the same route through the houseboat again and again. What I really want to do is something crazy, like convince the council to stop the traffic on the bridge in the middle of the night and see if that will get the whales home.

I wish Mom was here. I want to ask her what she would do. I want her to tell me Muncher will be okay. I want so much.

When I swing by the kitchen on one of my passes, there's a knock on the door. Startled, I glance at the time. One o'clock—school's not even out yet. . . .

I peek out the window, then open the door to Tal and a very wet Mut standing outside on the slippery dock.

"I stopped by Mud Bay and your father said you begged off school," he says in greeting. I grimace. Great. Dad knows I'm faking. Tal kicks off his shoes and steps inside wearing only his socks.

"A habit I picked up when I lived in Germany," he explains when he sees me notice. Mut sits waiting outside the door, whining. "Okay if he comes in?"

"Sure."

Mut bounds in, then stops to shake, sending water everywhere.

"Good timing," Tal laughs, settling himself at the counter. I open and close the cupboard, then the refrigerator, looking for something to offer him—tea, juice, anything. The place is a mess. Dirty dishes stacked in the sink. Grime and dried food stuck to the countertops. A pang of guilt runs through me again.

"Would you like a glass of water?" I ask, edging sideways toward the sink.

"Got enough of that out there, thanks," he says, nodding toward the window. "Fact of the Day—you think it's wet here? Would you believe that Seattle doesn't even make the Top 10 List for rainiest city in the US? Now if they picked the most *overcast* region, we'd have a shot to win, don't you think?"

There's an awkward silence while he waits for me to laugh but all I can manage is a weak smile. I wish I felt as hopeful as I did a few days ago, before Kevin brushed aside my discovery that it's the bridge stopping the whales from leaving, but I don't.

"Actually, Marisa, I stopped by because I have a favor to ask." When he sees my surprise he adds, "Yes, *you*. Only you, in fact."

I slide into the stool opposite, and wait.

"So, how do I put this? The 'No-Wake' hearing is Saturday night. I plan on attending and . . . " he hesitates, "I would like you to accompany me and let me add your name to the speaker list."

My eyes widen.

"You've been doing a tremendous job working with SoundKeeper to help the whales. I think it would behoove the council to hear your story in your own words."

I'm stunned. Me? Speak to the city council?

"I've already spoken to your father. He likes the idea, as does Dan O'Connor and Kevin."

At the mention of Kevin's name, I kick at the leg of my stool. Yeah, right. Actually, Kevin thinks my ideas are pretty lame.

"I think it might make a difference for the council to hear from a young person," he says. "They're a cantankerous bunch, and frankly there's about as much of a chance of their agreeing to close the inlet to vessel traffic as there is hope that the whales will sprout wings and fly home. But all we can do is try."

I smile at the image, but it only lasts a second, until I think about what he's really asking. "What would you want me to say?"

"It's not what *I* want you to say," Tal says. "It's what you feel you *need* to say. All I'm asking is that instead of keeping it all up here," he pokes at his forehead with his finger, "you share it with an audience. I think you're a fine young lady, Marisa, with a good, sensitive heart, and that speaks worlds to grumpy old men who might need a little nudge to take a chance." He looks at me gently. "Take it from a master. Right, Mut?"

At the sound of his name, Mut cocks his head and gives a little "woof." I want to say yes. It means a lot that Tal thinks I can do this. He's been so kind and helpful. Again, I can't help wondering about his daughter—why would she leave home, especially having a father like Tal? The thought ricochets right back at me, but I push it away and take a deep breath.

"Okay, I'll do it on one condition."

"Name it, ma'am."

I want to ask him about Carol Ann. I want to know what happened, and how he made peace with her leaving. But the words are stuck somewhere between my heart and my throat. Now is not the right time to try to make myself understandable.

Mut gives a loud yawn, and we both smile.

"When there's . . . time. . . . I have some questions, about something we have in common."

"That's it?"

I nod.

"Deal." He stands and slaps his thighs, smiling. "That's easy."

I smile back. Tal knows an awful lot, but this time I'm thinking he's wrong. Talking about losing someone you love won't be easy.

———

Tal isn't gone more than twenty minutes when Harris and Lena show up at the houseboat, with Jesse tagging along behind.

"Well, at least you haven't died," Lena says in greeting. "I thought after two days of letting your phone ring, we'd better check." Jesse immediately takes off, dead set on exploring every inch of the houseboat. "Are you ready to rejoin the land of the living?"

"Naomi sent us on a treasure hunt ... said you had a story to tell us about the whales," Harris says. "Whatever that means."

It's so good to see them both that pretty soon, without much coaxing, I'm telling the story of Muncher leading me back home two days ago on the inlet.

"You're sure you didn't imagine it?" Lena asks. "I mean, people imagine all sorts of things when they're scared."

I shake my head. "I didn't imagine it."

"Just a coincidence then?"

I shake my head again. "No, I know what I know."

Harris needs no convincing.

"Awesome! You tell anybody else?"

"Just Kevin and Naomi ... and you heard how that went."

"I don't know, Marisa. You oughta be telling *everybody*," Harris says. "Maybe the whales gave you this story for a reason."

Leave it to Harris to know how to make the best of a bad situation. Maybe he's right.

———

With extra urging from Jesse, I agree to go with Lena and Harris down to the boat launch. But the closer we get, the more I dread the idea of seeing Kevin after our last meeting.

"How's our whales doing?" Harris calls out as we near the parked orange van.

"Pretty vocal when we observed them this morning," Kevin answers, clicking his portable radio onto his belt. He nods to me, then climbs up inside to gather what he needs before heading out on the raft. "Not too many trips to the south end of the inlet, though. I think they're getting tired. We'll need to reassess the situation every day from here on."

I listen, feeling a weird mixture of embarrassment and impatience. To distract myself, I study the display of dorsal fin photographs that Kevin keeps spread out on his small table.

"I'm doing a fresh round of pictures tomorrow," he says when he sees me looking. "If anyone's interested."

"You bet!" Harris answers in a heartbeat. Playing outside the van, Jesse overhears. "You bet!" we hear him repeat.

Kevin waits for me to acknowledge his offer too, but I don't. I keep my eyes focused down at the table, at all the photos arrayed there. Each snapshot is small—no bigger than three by five inches. Kevin shoots close-ups with a telephoto lens, usually of the dorsal fins, saddle patches, and if he's lucky, the blowholes. At first, they all look the same. Only when I look more closely do I begin to see the subtle differences in color, pattern, and nick marks.

I pick up a few at random and flip them over, remembering Kevin's identification system.

L53 Lulu.

L90 Ballena.

L71 Hugo. I remember him—Rascal's brother, the next "sprouter."

L92 Crewser. Hey—Crewser! It's spelled differently, but I have to remember to tell Grace there's a whale with the same name as her father's boat.

L91 Muncher.

Muncher.

Kevin has joined me at the table and stands looking over my shoulder. There's a big stack of Muncher photos, all taken two days ago. "He hung around for a while so I got quite a few." I flip through the rest of the pile quickly, until one at the bottom makes me stop.

It's a photo of Muncher's upper body. I peer closer in the dim light of the van. Am I imagining it? No, there it is—a slight but definite depression around the edge of his blowhole.

My hand starts to tremble.

"Is this what you were telling us about? What happened to those whales up in Alaska?"

Kevin nods. "Nothing as extreme as that yet, but . . . a few are showing some weight loss. We'll keep evaluating."

"Which ones?"

"Ballena . . . and Kasatka."

I reach for Ballena's photos and sure enough, the same slight depression is visible.

"And a bit on Muncher." He clears his throat. "The younger ones are affected more quickly, like everything in life, I suppose."

I lay Ballena and Muncher's photos gently back down on the table and take a deep breath. Observe, reassess, evaluate. It's all just talk. No action.

Enough. I'm glad Kevin is being honest, not trying to cover up the danger, because it makes my decision that much easier.

———

Signaling that we need to go, I hustle Lena and Harris out of the van.

"We just got here! What's going on?" Harris demands as I lead them back along the shoreline road.

"We need to talk. *Now.* All of us. Grace too . . . I need everybody who's willing to help."

Jesse runs after us, struggling to keep up. "I'll help, Reesa!"

I slow down to give him a quick hug. "I know you will, Jesse. I can always count on you." He beams up at me and I take his hand to hurry him along. Twenty minutes later we're seated around the red Formica table at Garlic Jim's.

Harris drums his fingers on the table. "Talk," he orders.

"Okay." I take a deep breath. "We know the whales are in trouble but it's getting worse. They're tired, not surfacing as often, almost like they've given up. And they're starting to avoid the boats, even kayaks."

"It's true," Grace says. "Yesterday one of them breached three times near Daddy's kayak. It was weird . . . like a warning shot over the bow, right?" She looks at me and I nod, encouraged.

"But . . . even worse. I saw photos in Kevin's van just now. The little ones, Ballena and Muncher . . . and Grace, there's one called Crewser—"

"Really? Oh, how sweet!"

"Harris, remember those photos Kevin showed us of the whales that died up in Alaska? Ours are showing the same signs of shrinking around their blowholes." Harris's eyes widen with alarm. "We need to do something *now* . . . before it's too late. I have an idea but I need your help. I can't do this alone."

"Marisa . . . this is serious stuff. Are you sure you know what you're doing?"

I smile to myself. It's Lena—impulsive Lena urging *me* to be practical now. But she's right, I have to take her seriously.

"I know it's serious. . . ." I pause. "Don't worry, what I'm thinking isn't dangerous, just tricky."

She sighs but I see the slightest of smiles pulling at the corners of her mouth. "So . . . tell us your idea," she says, leaning forward.

"The city council meets Saturday, and Tal asked me to speak."

"Really?" Grace says, impressed.

"Cool!" Harris echoes.

"Naomi said once that to understand their behavior, you have to think like the whales. . . ." My friends stare at me, waiting. No one says a word. "So, if you're with me," I lower my voice, "here's what I'm thinking. . . .

CHAPTER 22

Orca Day 25

Our plan would be hard enough to pull off in good weather, but to complicate things it's been raining almost nonstop all week. On Friday afternoon, there's finally a break in the rain, but the weather report warns of an even bigger storm on the way. With the council meeting only one day away, it already feels too late. If my plan is going to work, we have to do it now—today—while we still have a window of relatively good weather.

I check my watch. It's already late, almost dinnertime. The front door slams and I quickly zip up my backpack and toss it in the corner. In the kitchen, Dad is pulling off his wet things and putting water on the stove for tea.

"It's nasty out there," he says, working at the heel of one of his waders with the toe of his other foot. I open the kitchen cabinet and pull out the box of tea bags.

"Any customers?"

"Not a lot. I think folks were a little put out by my refusal to rent on weekends." He grabs two mugs and pours in hot water. "So be it." He smiles. "I took a short tour of the inlet myself though, just to see what was up. Kept running into whales here and there . . .

never more than a couple in any one spot." He sits down at the counter and sighs. "They were scattered all over the place."

A memory triggers inside me. What was it Naomi said? If the pod is scattered around over a large area, something's usually up.

I take a seat across from Dad, dunking the tea bag up and down in the steaming liquid.

"Lena was wondering if I could spend the night with her at Grace's. They're working on a social studies assignment together . . . some kind of oral history thing, and they want to interview me." I try to keep my voice nonchalant, but it feels weird to be outright lying. "It's due Monday, but this weekend's going to be so busy. . . ."

"Grace's?" Dad raises his eyebrows at me from over his tea mug. "You two have gotten friendlier, haven't you?"

I shrug. "I guess. I think we just got tired of being mad at each other." The minute the words are out of my mouth, I know it's the truth. "So . . . is it okay? I can bike over."

"Sure. I'll miss you, of course." He stands up, leans over to kiss the top of my head, and then stretches, yawning. "I need a shower."

"Dad?"

He's halfway to the bathroom, and stops, waiting.

"What if Mom left . . . to try to find someone? Somebody important from a long time ago."

Dad makes a full turn. I can tell he's checking that he heard me right.

"I mean, if you knew that was why, would you have tried to stop her?"

Dad crosses his arms and leans back against the wall. "How do you know I didn't try?"

I blush, embarrassed to admit that, for all this time, I'd just assumed he hadn't. Then I remember that night... hearing Dad crying.

"Marisa, I've known your mother for a long time," he says. "But there's nothing she could have told me about her past, short of saying she was a murderer, that would make me turn away." A slight smile lightens his face. "She's family."

"But what if... I... I'm just so worried about...." My voice cracks and I stop.

Dad walks slowly back into the tiny kitchen and settles himself onto the stool opposite me at the counter.

"Listen to me." He reaches across and places both of his hands over mine, encircling the tea mug. "It's been hard for me to watch you in so much pain. But no one has forgotten you. *No one.*"

"No," I say, shaking my head. "That's not what I mean."

Dad thinks I'm talking about what's happening with Mom, and I am, but—it's more complicated. It's about belonging. It's about Mom *and* the orcas. Both have been connected from the very first moment these crazy whales entered the inlet.

"It's not about me anymore, Dad," I whisper. "There's more that...."

Dad waits for me to go on, but I can't tell him. Not yet. I know for sure now that he has no clue Mom had a baby before she met him, a baby she gave up when she probably wasn't much older than Carol Ann Reese.

How can I tell him that that baby's now grown up and found Mom, and she's gone to meet him? Because what if it doesn't work out? What if, after becoming a nurse and working with kids in those same kinds of situations, what if after all those years of trying to forget the hurt, she gets hurt even more? He sounded nice in his letter, but what if he really hates Mom for what she did? What if he only wanted to meet her to blame her?

What will happen then?

Dad still has his hands covering mine. We keep them entwined around my tea mug for a long time, holding on as if both of our lives depend on it.

———

Grace's house is bigger and fancier than I ever imagined, but there's no time now for a tour. Lena arrives and we order pizza, then hole up in Grace's room and set to work.

"There . . . that explains it really well," Lena says, holding up a legal size sheet of paper and admiring it. Harris's pictures of the orcas stare out at us above a paragraph I've written explaining the danger they're facing.

Grace leans over Lena's shoulder, and reads aloud: "We've all loved having the orcas here in the inlet, but now—for their own good—it's time for them to go home." That's cool. Now all we need to do is copy them.

We tramp single file down the hall of Grace's massive house and upstairs to her father's office. "The copy machine is in here," she whispers, opening the door. "Daddy lets me make copies when I need to, so this part is easy."

"Somehow," Lena says, "I don't think he was thinking you'd be making two *hundred* copies." But Grace just laughs.

"Oh well, whatever," she shrugs, smiling. "It's for a good cause."

———

That night, none of us can sleep, and it's a relief when the alarm buzzes just before four in the morning. We dress quickly and tiptoe around in the dark, gathering our supplies, then sneak out of Grace's house as quietly as we can, making our way down the long, winding path to the main road.

Harris is there waiting, just as we planned. "Hey, right on time," he says. "Thought maybe you'd change your mind. . . ." I hand him three of the nine grocery bags we've filled with the stacks of our flyers. "Okay, we've probably got three hours max to get these plastered all around the inlet. Let's go."

We set out first for Phinney Bay Marina, where Grace's father moors his boats. The road is deserted and we walk in silence. A thin drizzle is falling and the cold makes me shiver, but I'm grateful it's not pouring down rain.

"C'mon," Grace says as she pushes open the wooden gate and beckons for us to follow. Harris looks around the quiet marina. "No night guard?"

"Not in the winter. But maybe I shouldn't be telling *you* that," Grace whispers, but when I look at them, they're both laughing.

Working quickly, we load five of the bags of flyers into an old pickup truck that Grace's father keeps at the marina for dump runs. Then Grace leads us to the dock where her dad keeps an old motorboat moored and we stow the remaining four bags into the hull. Grace tosses a set of car keys to Harris, and she and Lena squeeze into what space is left in the motorboat.

"Okay," I say, "you guys head out and we'll follow in the truck. We'll meet at the bridge. Be careful. You're sure you're okay driving the boat?"

Grace waves me off. "Oh sure. I've made this run with Daddy so many times I could do it with my eyes closed. Hey, I *am* kind of doing it in the dark!" She giggles. "You're the one taking your life in your hands, riding in a truck with *him* driving!"

Grace starts the engine and the little motorboat rumbles to life. Harris and I wait until they're well out into the inlet. I check my watch. Almost five o'clock.

"Man, this is something," Harris whispers, as we walk back toward the marina in the dark. "We're really taking *action*." His words echo exactly what I've been feeling and reassure me that we're doing the right thing. The only sound is the gravel crunching under our feet.

"You think it's really gonna work?"

I turn away, not willing to tell him how nervous I am that what we're doing absolutely might not work, or might not matter in the end.

"It has to," I answer.

We climb into the truck. I wait, nervously drumming my hands on my knees, while Harris fiddles with the keys. "You sure you know how to do this?" I ask, rethinking the wisdom of this part of the plan.

"Yeah, yeah, no problem. Got a permit and everything."

He pats his wallet, but we both know he's not supposed to be driving alone, without an adult supervising. He turns the ignition again and a screeching metal sound erupts in the still air.

"Just not used to these trucks," he grins, nervous, and releases the clutch. I grip the door handle as the truck lurches out toward the shoreline road.

The eastern entrance to the bridge is busiest in the mornings, with workers commuting west, but at this hour on a Saturday, there's no one around. We stop every 100 feet, plastering every vertical pole we can find with our flyers, working as fast as we can. A thin fog is slowly rolling in from the mountains to the east. As we circle the inlet, I think about all the possible ways today can end.

Tal says what I say to the council members matters. Dad agrees. But what will possibly make a difference? What can even come close to what I'm feeling in my heart?

When I was little, Mom and I had this game that we made up

together that we called "What if . . ." We'd be out walking and we'd see a rabbit or a squirrel and one of us would ask the other, "What if the squirrel could talk? What if you could touch the clouds?" We could make up what if stories from any one tiny thing we saw.

Now my head is swirling with "What ifs?"

What if nobody reads our fliers?

What if all the whales die in the inlet?

Driving the dark inlet roads with Harris, tonight's speech on my mind, I play the "What if" game again and again.

What if things don't work out for Mom?

What if they do and she decides not to come back?

I lean back in the dark cab of the truck and sigh. Definitely not how the game was meant to be played.

CHAPTER 23

Orca Day 26

Five-thirty in the afternoon, a horn beeps sharply outside. It's Tal, come to pick me up for the meeting.

"You'll do fine," Dad says, giving me a hug. "I'll see you there."

When I open the door of Tal's truck, sitting in the backseat is Grace.

"Marisa," Tal greets me, "Grace will be joining us tonight." He glances at us, unsure how we'll react. "Her father's marina got hit pretty hard. I thought this might be something you two gals could see eye to eye on."

I climb in and nod. As we drive off, Grace and I share a secret smile.

———

Tal needs to circle the streets around the County Annex Building three times before he can find a parking spot. With six blocks to walk, I take deep breaths of the cool night air, trying to calm down. We're just about to enter the building when Tal stops me with a look.

"You, my dear . . ." he says, then glances at Grace, smiling, "and your friends . . . you make me very proud of young people today. You give me hope. Don't worry, you'll do just fine." He turns to walk up the steps.

Now, I decide. Now is the time to ask him.

"I know about your daughter," I call out. Tal turns and looks at me sideways.

"Yes, I know you know," he says softly. Behind us, a car honks past.

"I wanted to ask. . . . " Tal waits, and I swallow. "After she left . . . did you ever wish you'd done anything differently? I . . . I'm not saying you did anything wrong, but still, there must have been something—" I stop, embarrassed.

Tal takes off his cap, scratches his head, and says one word: "Mut."

"I . . . I don't understand. . . ." Is he telling me I should get a dog?

"Mut," he repeats. "It's the German word for 'courage.' The thing is, Marisa . . . it's very easy to blame ourselves, for all kinds of things that are out of our control." He exhales and I know he's trying to decide how to explain. "I'm not denying I was partly to blame. But blame only leads to anger, and anger takes an awful lot of energy. It will eat you up inside if you let it."

He pauses and I wait for more. At my side, Grace doesn't say a word, but I feel her arm slide around my waist.

"Not a day goes by that I don't look up and expect to see her. Every day. And maybe I will someday. So better to forgive. Forgiveness is a choice too, Marisa. But forgiveness takes courage. Because it's not just the person who hurt you that you're forgiving, you also need to forgive yourself. The change needs to be inside *you*. And the only way that can happen is if you grow in courage. And that can take a very long time. Do you understand what I'm saying?"

I nod and look down at my feet. "I think so."

"Giving Mut his name was one more way for me to sustain my courage," Tal tells me. "*You* have that courage, Marisa, I can see it in you. The courage to handle whatever happens with your mother. To handle what you're about to do now."

It's strange. I thought my questions were just about me. But listening to Tal, maybe I was asking about Mom, too. Maybe she needed this time, just like Tal, to work up the courage to forgive herself.

I'm trying to make sense of it all, when Tal reaches into his pocket and holds out his hand to me. Lying there in his palm is Carol Ann's shiny charm bracelet. The blue glass eyes of the leaping orca sparkle under the streetlights.

"Bette asked me to give it to you when the time seemed right. I'd say that would be just about now. She says you and your mother are both made of the same mettle. *Mettle*: courage, and strength of character," Tal says, giving me the answer this time.

My eyes are stinging and I don't dare look at Tal or I'm afraid I'll burst into tears.

"Thanks," I whisper. "You can always ask for it back." Grace gives me a little squeeze and I slip the bracelet on my wrist.

"Now . . ." Tal says, giving me a smile, "show your mettle. Go get 'em!"

———

Inside, the meeting has already started. As we hurry in, a fresh wave of anxiety rises inside me when I look around the packed room. I was expecting a small-town gathering like the ones at the Sons of Norway. This is different . . . bigger . . . way more official.

"Hey!" Grace nudges me, "the flyers worked!"

There must be hundreds of people here, with more streaming in behind us. There are no open seats anywhere. We worm our way into an open spot at the side, maneuvering as close to the front as we can. Up on the stage, the county representatives—six men and two women—are seated at two long tables facing the audience. Each has a nameplate placard and microphone in front of them. Two whiteboards stand behind the table—one lists the meeting's agenda, the other, the order of speakers.

There it is, third from last, my name—*Marisa Gage.*

A woman dressed in a dull blue business suit stands speaking at the podium.

"Who's that?" Grace whispers.

"County commissioner," Tal answers, "one of them anyway."

Clustered near us are news reporters and photographers. I hear the whirring click of expensive cameras.

The county commissioner continues, "You can be assured that both city and county officials are working together closely on this matter."

"I don't think they expected this much of a turnout," Tal says, looking around.

"We did it!" Grace leans over and whispers.

I nod numbly, shifting my weight uneasily back and forth from one foot to the other. My mind just keeps replaying what I need to say when it's my turn.

For close to an hour we listen, as one speaker after another drones on. One man talks about all the extra business the whale watchers are bringing to the area. A woman who lives near the ferry terminal is all worked up about the long lines of cars backed up into her neighborhood. All the while, more people stream into the room until the guards stop them at the door and those who are turned away have to spill out into the hallway.

Dad must be here somewhere but I don't see him. I fidget with my notes. The sheet of paper is nearly in shreds. I try to concentrate on what the speakers are saying but it's useless.

Finally, it's time.

———

"Our next speaker is Marisa Gage." My name echoes out over the crowd. "Will you come forward, please?"

I feel a pat on my back from Tal as I squeeze past him. "Good luck!" Grace whispers. My legs wobble slightly as I climb the steps and walk across the stage. I reach the podium and turn to face the crowd.

"Hello," I speak into the microphone, "Tal Reese asked me to talk to you tonight." My voice is carried, amplified, out over the audience, and I'm reminded again of the underwater vocalizations of the whales. "I live on a houseboat that was nearly wrecked by the fast wakes of the big vessels that have been speeding into the inlet to see the whales."

Errrrrreeeee—

A screech of feedback erupts from the microphone, making me jump. A second later, the noise fades, and it takes something else along with it. Maybe it's because the lights trained on the stage are so bright I can't see anyone's face, or maybe my adrenaline kicks in like Mr. O'Connor says it will when we give our science reports.

For whatever reason, I stare into the shadowy shape of the audience spread out before me and lose all my fear. I'm still me, standing there in front of all these people—scientists, reporters, officials, and my neighbors—but now I know *exactly* what I want to say. I don't even bother looking down at the crumpled paper in my hand. All that matters now is that I tell my story. When the feedback fades, I begin.

"I was going to tell you the story of how the wakes damaged my houseboat. But I've changed my mind. That's not really important." I can feel the audience's attention sharpen. "If that's all we try to fix, maybe the boats will slow down, but that won't solve the real problem, which is figuring out how to get our whales back home where they belong."

And from that beginning, I speak with quiet confidence, telling the audience how the whales are in grave danger. I tell the story of Barnes Lake and how some of the whales there died of starvation. I explain how Muncher and some of the other young whales are beginning to show signs of malnutrition.

At some point, I realize I'm not talking to the crowd anymore. I'm telling my story of the last three weeks to someone else, someone much more important than anyone out there in the dark hall. Someone I desperately want to know what's happening.

I squeeze my eyes shut against the bright lights, and imagine . . .

There! I can see her clearly now in my mind, as if she really were here. She's sitting a few rows back, hands crossed in her lap, smiling. And she's listening. She can *hear* me.

"Mom?" Did I actually say her name out loud?

"You've got their hearts now, Marisa," she whispers. "Good girl. I knew you could do it."

"Should I tell them about the kayak in the fog?"

"It's your choice," she says. "But I would. It's an important story. Remember, they need to experience it as you did."

I can feel the audience getting restless. Just one second more.

I rub the little orca charm on Carol Ann's bracelet, take a deep breath, and open my eyes. For the next few minutes, I share what it felt like to "hear" the tremendous noise of the bridge when I was under it in my kayak. I explain what Naomi taught me about sound being amplified underwater, how the roar of an engine can frighten and disorient orcas, especially the young ones, who are so sensitive.

I describe seeing the mother orcas making their exit but then turning back because the calves wouldn't follow. It's simple to understand why they'd do that, isn't it?

I know I don't have much more time—I can see the announcer checking his watch. My voice gets stronger, louder. I don't need the microphone at all when I announce proudly that it was my friends and I who posted the flyers around the inlet. That's why there are hundreds of people here tonight. And then I tell them we have no choice—we have to do something.

"The whales are trapped. And we can't waste any more time . . . we have to take action now. Please, tell the county commissioners to close the Warren Avenue Bridge to traffic. It's the only chance the whales may have to get safely home. The only other option is watching them starve to death and die . . . right here in Dyes Inlet."

Then it's over and I rush off the stage to thunderous applause. The sound follows me as I step into the darkness of the hall and stumble my way back to Tal and Grace.

Harris and Lena have made their way over, applauding wildly. My adrenaline fades and I feel like I've just run a sprint. Naomi runs up to give me a hug. When I turn to look for Dad, he's right there with a big grin on his face. He opens his arms wide, and I fall into them gratefully, his warmth silencing my shaking body.

Once more, I close my eyes. And I see her again. She's standing and clapping now, along with the rest of the audience. I imagine someone next to her now, too—a young man in his twenties. He's got the same thick, dark hair as Mom and me.

Both of them are smiling.

CHAPTER 24

Orca Day 28

*A*ll day Sunday and Monday we wait, and hope, until finally, late in the evening we get the good news. The county commissioners announce that they've approved the request to set up a "No-Wake Zone" for any vessels entering through the Narrows. Even better, they vote 5-2 to close the Warren Avenue Bridge to all traffic except emergency vehicles for a twenty-four-hour period, and to restrict boat traffic on the inlet to approved vessels only.

"Yahoo!" I cheer when Dad hangs up the phone and shares the details with me.

"That was the *Inlet News*. Apparently, the county offices were flooded with calls and e-mails yesterday. The story will be on the front page of tomorrow's edition," Dad tells me. He's grinning, actually grinning, from ear to ear. "And it's all because of you."

"Not just me, Dad. My friends helped a ton."

Not to mention a little help from Mom, too. But I can't stop smiling. We did do it, didn't we?

The commissioners schedule the bridge closure for Wednesday morning to give people time to make other plans for their commutes. Wednesday is two long days away, and everyone gets busy planning.

All the whales need to do is hold out a little longer.

———

It's been a long few days, and I just can't wait another minute. After dinner on Tuesday, I turn off all the lights except the small one over the stove, then I pull the blue envelope out from my pocket. Pushing aside some dirty teacups and take-out food containers, I gently slide out the letter and leave it sitting there for a minute on the kitchen counter.

How old is the writer, I wonder. Older than Carol Ann Reese? Will he say where he lives now and what he's doing? Will he ask if Mom has any other kids?

There's only one way to find out.

"Dad?"

"Umm?" He walks into the kitchen, toweling dry his hair after a late-night shower.

"There's a letter here I think we should read. Together."

His eyes flicker to the envelope lying on the countertop, then back to me.

"From Mom?"

I shake my head no. Unfolding the sheet of paper, I smooth it out flat on the counter. Dad sits down beside me. I feel his arm encircle my shoulders and together, we begin to read.

Dear Mrs. Gage,

After mailing you my first letter, I panicked. I'm guessing you've received it by now and are probably still in shock that the son you gave up for adoption years ago has contacted you. With all my heart, I hope that you decide to contact me at the phone number I provided. But if you can-

not or do not want to ever meet me in person, there are a few things I don't want to leave unsaid.

Because giving you my name and phone number isn't the same as telling you what my life has been like.

So here goes. . . .

My adoptive parents, Craig and Brenda, are wonderful. They named me Ben. And I had an older sister, Gina, but she died when she was thirteen, in a car accident when she was staying with friends. It was so sad, I hardly got to know her. We lived in North Hollywood, but after Gina's death, when I was eight, we moved to Bakersfield.

What else? When I was a kid, I loved to swim. I swam all the time. Was on swim teams for almost ten years, and I was pretty good! As a teenager I worked as a lifeguard and taught swim lessons to kids. I still swim a couple of days a week at the local Y.

I guess my absolute favorite thing to do these days is go up into the mountains. Camping, fishing, hiking—you name it, I do it.

I just finished up my degree in Mathematics and Natural Science at CSU Bakersfield. I graduate this June. I'm hoping to get a job as an environmental biologist. Cross your fingers!

I guess that's enough about me. I'm hoping to meet you someday so we can get to know each other better. For now, I just want you to know that I'm okay. And I hope you're okay, too. I have a good life and I don't hate you for what you did.

Your son, Ben

———

I keep my eyes on the counter, where Ben's letter lies open, nervous about Dad's reaction. Because even though Dad is Dad, I know this is huge.

"It must have been hard," he says finally, breaking the silence. "For both of them. Stepping into each other's lives like that."

"How are you feeling?" I ask.

"Well . . ." he lets out a long breath, "life isn't always a straight line. It twists and turns and changes. We do our best to make a plan, but at the end of the day, it's our choice. I think there's enough love to go around, don't you?"

He picks up Ben's letter, folds it back up, and hands it to me.

"Ben," Dad says, smiling. "I think she'll like that name."

CHAPTER 25

Orca Day 30

At the set time—seven o'clock in the morning on Wednesday, November 19—two Port Washington police officers park their vehicles, blocking the east and west entrances of the Warren Avenue Bridge. The officers unload barricades and set them up across the entrance ramp, propping a "Road Closed" sign against it. They flip the flasher light to the "on" position, and the still-dark road glows with amber light.

Instantly, the span is totally and officially closed.

"I'm still in shock," Kevin says, shaking his head. "For once, the vote came down on the side of the orcas, instead of the humans."

We've all gathered just off the bridge deck to watch. For a few minutes, we celebrate. Then reality sets in and we realize we have precious little time to help the orcas leave, and yet there's so little we can control. Almost everything depends on luck.

Some of our ideas Kevin vetoed as too stressful for the whales, including making loud noises or lining the channel with boats to herd the whales in the right direction. So the approved plan includes playing recorded whale sounds to entice the whales out, keeping our vessels in position to block their return, and gently coaxing them southward with back-and-forth passes.

We've also loaded the motorboat with close to two hundred pounds of salmon—just a snack, really, for nineteen orcas. They won't eat fish that have been dead for too long, but the scent alone should be good enough to lure them. All we really want is to attract the whales to the end of the inlet.

Secretly, I'm really praying the whales will know what to do all on their own.

"Twenty-four hours," Naomi whispers. "Let's make it count."

"What are y'all waiting for?" Kevin says. "Let's go!"

———

We scramble down to where the raft is prepped and waiting. Harris and I jump in and Kevin takes off. Lena, Grace, and Naomi follow behind in the motorboat as we cruise out toward the open water of the inlet to see if we can locate the pod. The Suquamish Tribe has sent a single, large canoe, with about a dozen rowers, to paddle alongside our vessels. Most look young—no more than seventeen or eighteen—and I wonder how they were selected for this assignment.

"I was out early this morning," Kevin shouts over the noise of the engine. "The whales were scattered all over the place!"

A dark purple-gray cloud cover hangs low over the inlet. Off in the distance, to the west, there's just the barest strip of sky visible at the base of the horizon. The wind whips my hair around as we speed across the water, leaving the bridge behind.

We reach the center of the inlet, and Kevin kills the motor. Nearby, Grace's motorboat rumbles to a stop. Naomi drops the hydrophone over the side, except this time, instead of recording the whales, we're transmitting prerecorded vocalizations, hoping to lure the pod in the direction of the bridge.

"These calls are from L Pod, so we've got a better shot at them working than they did up in Alaska," Naomi says, biting her lip. "Hopefully, it'll get their attention. Still . . . these guys are so darn smart. . . ."

We wait. Water sloshes around the raft as we bob in the water. The whales are nowhere to be seen. Half an hour later, the tape ends. Naomi clicks rewind and the audio starts up again.

Where could they be? Did they just decide to hole up somewhere and sleep the day away? Lifting the binoculars, I scan back and forth across the wide expanse of the inlet.

Then I see them.

"Naomi, there!" I call out, pointing south, back toward Rocky Point. Off in the distance, I can just make out vague clouds of whale blows rising from the surface.

"And there," Naomi repeats, pointing west now, toward Chico Bay. I look and see birds diving at the water surface. She swivels her head 180 degrees. "And there!"

"They're milling. . . ." Kevin murmurs, swiveling to check out each location. "Turning to move in the same direction." He turns to Naomi. "Okay, let's back 'em up, make sure they don't do an about-face. Follow me!"

We speed south, toward the bridge, taking care to stay well behind the whales but positioning our two crafts so that any of the groups would have to pass directly by us to head back north into the inlet. Within five minutes we're smack in the middle of the three groups. They've slowed now, each grouping no more than forty feet away in any direction. We kill our engines and hunker down, waiting to see what they decide to do next.

The group to the west consists of most of the big guys. As we watch, they make a run at the surface, swimming fast as a group, their bodies almost touching, and a huge wall of water blocks them from our view. Then in a flash, they change direction. There's some breaching and tail slaps, but most of the activity is underwater. Then the whale Kevin identifies as L26, Baba, turns onto her side and starts pec slapping the water.

"I've seen her do that before when she gets near the bridge!" I shout out, remembering that day up in Tal and Bette's tower. "I think she's trying to get the others motivated!"

I spot Kevin's foam-lined camera case lying on the floor of the raft near my feet. Without even asking, I reach down and grab it, then heave the thing over the side, and start slapping the water with it, imitating Baba's movement. The case is light but almost the size of a small briefcase, and it makes a satisfying *smack—smack—smack* on the water's surface.

"Maybe a little backup will help her motivate them," I say when Naomi stares at me like I've lost my mind. She hesitates a second, then grabs a life jacket and does the same. But Baba just looks at us curiously. The other whales ignore us completely. Apparently our pec slaps are not very motivating.

For the next hour we try everything we can think of to urge the whales on. Nothing works. A little more than 2,000 feet ahead, the hulking mass of the bridge looms, silent at last. Twice, a group makes an approach, and we throw salmon out as a lure, but each time they turn back. And every time they do, Kevin and Grace maneuver to partially block them from making a full retreat back into the inlet.

By noon, all three groups are still holding their positions, milling around but not seeming to want to go anywhere in particular. The tribal paddlers in the canoe don't seem bothered by the wait, they're relaxed and chatting, but the rest of us are exhausted.

"How long can they keep this up?" I ask Kevin.

He starts to answer when, suddenly, the hydrophone picks up something weird. Some kind of signal, something deliberate, passes among the three groups of whales. We all hear it. They begin chirping, first one group, then the second, then the third . . . it repeats and cycles, going on and on until the individual sounds all blend together.

Alongside us, the paddlers in the canoe are suddenly on high alert. One young man sounds his drum with short, sharp beats, while the others ready their paddles.

"Whoa . . . this is kind of eerie," Harris says, shifting his weight in the raft. One after another, a dozen whales stick their heads up out of the water, spyhopping. Some follow with a tail slap, a roll, or a breach for good measure.

I watch, fascinated, feeling the electricity passing between them. They're communicating. And something else, too. . . .

"I know it sounds crazy, but . . ." I whisper, "but it's almost like they're *arguing*."

Harris laughs. "Nothing would surprise me about these whales."

We're really close to the bridge now. I can feel the current pulling our raft out toward the mouth of the inlet. I notice how quiet it is. With the roar of bridge traffic gone, the air is absolutely silent.

"There!" Kevin yells. He points ahead to where a huge whale has positioned himself at the top point of the triangle that the three groups have formed. A hissing sound surrounds us, growing louder and louder. "L57 . . . Faith! He's taking the lead!"

I swivel around to see. All the whales are blowing rapidly now in synchronization, five or six times each. Short, quick breaths fill the air.

Pfoosh—Pfoosh—Pfoosh.

At the same time, they close ranks until the whole pod is now one huge group assembling directly ahead of us.

"What's happening?" Harris yells.

"They're getting ready to dive!" I shout.

"And it's gonna be one heck of a deep one!" Kevin announces.

The blows continue, rapid and short, with the last ending in one long exhaled breath. Finally, a great *whooshing* noise echoes around us as nineteen whales, in unison, dive one final time, sending the water around our raft roiling and bucking.

"Whoa!" Kevin yells. He turns on the motor, struggling to hold the craft steady against the enormous pull the pod's dive has created. "I'm gonna follow!" he shouts and we take off like a shot. I hear the rumble of Grace's motorboat coming to life as she struggles behind us, bucking in the current. Somehow, the tribal canoe keeps up, the paddlers pulling hard in the water while two continue drumming.

We cross under the bridge. The deck is jammed with people above, all peering down at the water. Kevin quickly guides our raft to the right, hugging the western shore, to give the pod the full width of the inlet to maneuver. He positions us so that we're looking north under the bridge again back into Dyes Inlet. In Grace's motorboat, Naomi counts dorsal fins as they slice past us through the water.

"Are they all through?" I shout, turning to her.

"Just about," she yells back. "Seventeen so far!"

The water under the bridge is empty now at the surface but churning underneath. As the whales pass through, they spread out widely into Rich Passage, slowly riding each other's waves and the tidal current.

I look back under the bridge just in time to see one lone whale breach, shooting herself straight up into the air. Then—spectacularly—half a dozen whales on our side of the bridge breach off our starboard side, led off by Canuck, breaking the surface not more than twenty feet from our raft.

"They're starting to party!" Harris yells over the din. Up on the bridge deck, seeing the majority of the whales passing by, people start to whoop and holler.

"They're gonna make it!" Kevin says. Tears are streaming down his face. "They're *really* gonna make it."

Near the bridge, on the inlet side, two whales remain, circling. The tribal drummers start up a steady beat again.

"Look!" I shout, pointing, "it's Muncher!"

Kevin brings his binoculars up to check as the little one does a spyhop.

"You're right," he nods. "Looks like he's got his mom with him ... L47, Marina."

Out already in the passage, Canuck heaves herself up out of the water again, breaching, offering encouragement. Still in the inlet, Marina gives a deep blow and dives under the bridge. I hold my breath with her, waiting for Muncher to follow.

"C'mon Muncher, you can do it," I whisper as much to myself as to the little calf.

After what feels like an eternity, Muncher blows and dives. Immediately I scan the water beyond the bridge, waiting for him to surface next to Marina. Where is he? I can't tell ... he's been submerged for so long.

Then I see him, and my heart leaps into my throat. He's circling—still in the inlet! It looks like he's resting, almost drifting on the surface. In a trance, I watch Muncher circling ... circling ... circling. It seems to last forever, until at last, Muncher sends up a big blow. I watch in horror as his mother, Marina, swims under the bridge to join him—back into the inlet.

CHAPTER 26

I stand in the raft, staring, frozen. What just happened? I can't believe it! Not again.

We have to do something, quickly. *Now.* The other whales are farther out now, behind me, in Sinclair Inlet, but once they notice Marina and Muncher are missing, they might come back.

"We need to go get them!" I shout to Kevin, but immediately he shakes his head.

"We've gotta stay right here," he shouts back. "We need to block any from returning!"

I stare at him, not understanding.

"Come on, we'll take you," a voice says, startling me. I turn to see one of the young men, one of the drummers, in the canoe. His voice is impossibly soft but somehow I can hear his words loud and clear. He nods, and I know he's beckoning me over. Without hesitation, I grab the extra paddle lying on the raft's floor, and using it for leverage, I leap across the water into the front of his canoe.

"Marisa! What in blazes—" I hear Kevin shout behind me, but it's too late.

"We're the fastest paddlers," the soft-spoken drummer

announces, smiling, as his companions begin to pull with their paddles.

We make extraordinary time. In less than a minute, we're back under the bridge and fifty yards into the inlet, close to where Marina and Muncher silently circle.

They see us.

"Look how beautiful they are," the drummer says. He beats out five slow, steady beats on his drum.

Marina is heading straight for our canoe now. Does she recognize me from our meeting in the fog when she led me to safety? Does she know I'm trying to help? She's so focused on Muncher I hope she doesn't think I'm threatening him. I have to get her attention, make her watch *me*, instead of Muncher, convince her that we both want the same thing.

I swivel around. The current and tides are still moving fast; I can feel its pull on our canoe. Orcas ride the tides, surf a vessel's wake sometimes. It's now or never.

I pick up my paddle, and with all my strength, bring it down hard on the surface of the water—*slap—slap—slap*. At the same time, I concentrate, willing Marina to read my mind. The paddle is heavy, and my arms start to ache, but I keep it up, until finally, Marina brings up her fin and slaps the water in reply.

Once. Twice. On the third slap Muncher joins in.

Soon the three of us are slapping happily away. A minute later, Muncher sends a spout of fine steam into the air, and follows up with a long, shrill whistle, *Oooooooooeeeeeee!*

"A good omen," the young drummer says. Without turning to look, I can tell he's smiling. He brings a small, silver whistle to his lips and answers the call. *Oooooooooeeeeeee!*

The paddlers begin to stroke, pulling the canoe back toward

the bridge, speeding us along. I take a quick peek over my shoulder and see Marina and Muncher alongside. They're following us! They understood!

In unison, they blow—*pfooosh*—*pfoosh*—*pfoosh*—at least six in a row, maybe more, short and fast, and ending with one long breath. In the canoe, I take a deep breath too, inhaling wholeness and change, and exhaling everything that's been holding me back, keeping me stuck.

Five powerful strokes later, we pass under the bridge and out of the inlet, the last whales cruising behind us in our wake.

———

Kevin does a final check to be sure all the whales have passed through. Just to be safe, the canoe floats parallel to the bridge, Kevin sets his raft dead center under the bridge deck, and Grace does the same with the motorboat. We're not taking any chances.

Out in Rich Passage, we can see the entire pod moving through the water fast now, at super high speed. It's called *porpoising*. Their bodies arch above the surface, then dip down below so quickly that it looks like they're barely touching the water.

Kevin laughs. "I think they just found dinner!"

"Man! They're chowing down!" Harris yells. "The inlet must be cleaned out."

Watching, I don't even try to find the words to express what I'm feeling. In the chill water of the inlet, a deep warmth fills me when I see Muncher and his mother swim over to rejoin their group. Side by side they roll and breach, eating, playing, enjoying their new freedom. We stay until the whole pod is far out of sight, well past the Port Washington waterfront and far out into Sinclair Inlet.

Kevin is just about to turn us fully around when L57, Faith, swims back toward us. His huge six-foot fin arches high out of the water before he dives, surfacing one last time a few yards away. Then, with a wave of his dorsal fin, he's gone.

"Good-bye," I whisper to the still-churning water.

I miss them already.

CHAPTER 27

Thursday, morning breaks gray and hazy over the steely water of the inlet. I wake early, restless after yesterday's excitement of escorting the whales out under the bridge on their way home. Piling sweaters on, I wander down the dock. There's a clear view of the Narrows and the channel beyond and I sit on the damp wood of the dock, hugging my knees in the cool morning air. Above, a hawk wheels in a circle, scanning for breakfast.

The water is calm, with hardly a ripple across the surface. For close to four weeks, I've gotten used to seeing the whales here every day. It became so easy to forget they really belonged somewhere else. Now that they're gone, the inlet seems empty without them.

In the distance, the Warren Avenue Bridge is humming again with traffic. I'm sure of it even though I'm not close enough to hear. How odd that it turned out to be a bridge that blocked the orcas from leaving. Bridges are supposed to connect, but they can separate and divide, too. I guess it all depends on your perspective, and which side you're on.

———

At school, classes seem like an interruption of one long conversation. Except for science, where it's always okay to talk about whales.

"My guess is if they visit again, there won't be quite as much reason to worry—" Mr. O'Connor is saying. He's interrupted by a knock on the door and Kevin and Naomi walk in carrying four large boxes of donuts.

"Lunchtime!" Kevin announces and the class goes wild.

"We just want to say thank you for all the help y'all have provided these four weeks," he says, walking among the desks offering the contents of the open boxes. "You should feel very proud of yourselves." He stops near my desk, smiles, and offers me a glazed donut. I take a bite and it's the sweetest thing I've ever tasted.

Later in the hallway, Naomi reaches out and gives Harris, Lena, and Grace each a big hug. When it's my turn, she holds on a second longer.

"Thank you *so* much," she whispers.

It feels good. Belonging again.

"Hey, listen," she says, her voice brighter, "anytime you guys want to come up to the islands, you have a place to stay." She raises her voice over our yelps of excitement, "And you have to come visit L Pod, so no excuses!"

"You, young man," I overhear Kevin say to Harris, "have quite an eye for the camera. You should pursue that."

Harris beams and pumps Kevin's hand. "Thanks, man. I already am."

"Enough already," Lena kids him, tugging on Harris's arm. "He's gonna get a big head."

"Science to the rescue!" Mr. O'Connor shouts, breaking up the crowd. "I'm escorting them to the ferry. Scatter! Scatter!"

As we wave our last good-byes, Lena turns to me.

"Coming to Garlic Jim's?"

I shake my head. "I think I'm going to head home. I've got a bunch of stuff to do."

She smiles and gives me a hug. "You're just lucky I'm not so worried about you anymore. I'll call later."

I bike the long way home, not wanting to give up my view of the inlet just yet. It rained hard last night, but now the roads are dry and I glide out on my usual route. Except this time, when I pass the high school field, I turn right and head north instead of south.

Tracyton Boulevard is almost empty. I catch glimpses of the inlet sparkling through openings between the trees, still water with no boats in sight. I slow when I reach the place where the road curves and intersects the Clear Creek Trail. Veering south, I skirt the town of Silverdale, skidding my bike to a stop at the mouth of Chico Creek. The water is green and slimy at the edge and smells like rotting fish. The chum run still has a couple more weeks to go but most of the returning salmon have done their duty. They're back home, to the place where they were spawned, to lay their eggs and begin the cycle of life again.

On a whim, I pull out my water bottle and dip it into the cold murky water of the creek. It fills halfway with grit and slime, and I screw the lid back on and replace it on my bike bracket. The whales are on their way home, and I suddenly want something they've touched, something to remind me of their thirty-day visit. Circling the whale-less inlet, I renew my resolve to be like Muncher—to trust.

It takes me about an hour to reach Veneta Street and the marina. I'm tired and thirsty but haven't felt this peaceful in a long time. I push against the door of the houseboat. It opens easily.

"Dad?" I call, stepping inside.

"Right here." Dad walks into the kitchen, carrying a cup of tea and a newspaper. I move toward him and give him a hug.

"You okay?"

"Yeah," I reassure him, and it's true. "I'm just going to miss them, I think."

Dad stares at me, silent, but I see his eyebrows go up.

"What?"

Dad hands me a slip of paper with a phone number scribbled on it. "Mom asked if you'd call her back." He smiles. "She says she has some good news."

I take the scrap of paper and fold my palm over it. Then Dad opens a drawer under the kitchen counter and pulls out a thick stack of mail, held together with a wide rubber band.

"I think you might want these, too," he says, holding them out toward me.

"What are they?" I pull off the band, frowning. All the letters are in Mom's handwriting, addressed to me but mailed to Dad at the Mud Bay Kayak address. "Wait . . . how did Mom *know*?"

"She suspected you'd tossed her first few letters, so she sent all the rest to me, to hold them for you until you were ready." He grins. "When your mother sets her mind on something, there's no stopping her. Kind of like somebody else I know and love."

"Thanks, Dad . . . for everything. I love you." I walk to my room and shut the door as quietly as I can.

———

Clicking on the radio, I tune in to my favorite alternative rock station and climb up on my bed. At first, I get that familiar feeling of dread, thinking of what the letters might contain, but it doesn't last. Everything is different now—the whole mood of what I'm about to do has changed.

Sitting cross-legged, I cradle the stack in my lap. Some of the envelopes are thin, others bulging fat. I have to smile. Mom trusted me. She knew I'd want these eventually, and I'm so grateful to have them now. Spread out on my bed in chronological order, they make me think of the photos of the whales in Kevin's van.

Slowly, I count them.

Twenty letters, more than I thought. Twenty. Almost as many days as the whales had been in the inlet.

I open all the envelopes at once and lay the letters out, smoothing the sheets of paper on my bed. Eager, I reach for one with an early date. I scan it quickly and move on to the next. My heart is filling quickly with so much emotion that it feels close to bursting.

Slow down. Slow down. But I can't. I skim them all, jumping around the paragraphs, not understanding everything, but absorbing the most important bits. When I finish one, I reach immediately for the next, like a starving person who's finally been offered a plate of food.

... I hope my letters will help you understand, at least a little. It's really important for me to be completely honest with you, but first I needed to be honest with myself....

... M, you have a brother. I am so sorry it's taken me so long to tell you about him. It's a long story, one that I made your father swear never to ask me about....

I made lots of mistakes. I was seventeen, living in a house with my parents but really, I was all alone. I was so confused, hurting, no one I could talk to.... Two months later I found out I was pregnant....

... I was a total mess. I knew there was no way I could take care of a baby. I thought maybe it would be better to just end the pregnancy right then and there. But when I walked out toward the bay I saw a pod of

humpbacks. I don't know why, but watching them gave me hope. I decided to have the baby and give it up for adoption. So in a way, the whales are responsible for Ben being here today. . . .

. . . I've finally met Ben, your brother! I made it through the whole first meeting without totally losing it. He's a wonderful, wonderful young man. I'm so in awe of his accomplishments, grace and courage. M, you're going to LOVE him when you meet. . . .

. . . I'll be home soon, sweetie. I can see the light at the end of the tunnel. But, maybe with your help, I'll wind up free—on the other side.

It takes me close to two hours to make my way through all of them. When I'm finally finished, I'm exhausted, exhilarated and weepy all at the same time. A whole new chapter has been added to my life. I have an older brother! He's well and happy, and best of all he's forgiven my mother. And so have I.

So much has changed since she left. I've learned so much. About myself, about Mom and the importance of family, about what it means to be connected. Slowly a new feeling fills me.

I'm proud of her.

I understand now that she needed to leave to save herself. But she didn't leave me alone. Somehow she sent the whales to me. They came when I needed them, I know that in my heart. And I'm stronger now, the way she wanted me to be. I have *mut* . . . the courage to believe, to trust, and to fight for what I want and make it happen.

Next summer, when the whales follow the salmon run again, I'll be thirteen. It feels as if a whole new world is opening up.

The day is gone. The window near my bed is slightly open and the sounds of nighttime on the inlet drift in toward me—the soothing splash of slow water, the drone of a ship's horn. Through the smudged glass, the small, bright orb of the moon is beginning its rise over the inlet. I rouse myself and rummage around the cluttered bed until I find what I'm looking for. In the time it takes me to punch in the ten-digit number scribbled on the slip of paper Dad gave me, the moon climbs in the sky to fill the frame of my tiny window, illuminating the water of the inlet and the dim outline of the Warren Avenue Bridge in the distance.

The ringing, faraway but insistent, reaches deep down inside me, bringing with it a whole new set of feelings. In the dim light of the houseboat, I hear more in that ringing than I could ever have imagined. I hear the sound of ferries and foghorns; the drum beats of the Coast Salish tribes; and the reassuring whistle of a mother whale summoning her wayward calf. I listen and seem to hear clearly the sound of courage, the sound of choosing to love, choosing to take control of your life.

Finally, the ringing stops.

"Hello?"

"Mom! It's me! I have SO much to tell you. But first, remember the whale watching trip you've been wanting to plan? Next spring, when the whales come home, I think we should all go." And there in the dark, I close my eyes and take that leap of faith. "You, me, Dad . . . and Ben."

AUTHOR'S NOTE

Chasing at the Surface is a novel, and its characters and situations are fictional, although some place-names have been borrowed and much of the genealogy and science behind the study of killer whales is authentic. What is perhaps most interesting is that the backstory for this book is based on a true event.

The actual story goes like this. In the fall of 1997, nineteen Southern Resident killer whales (SRKW), members of L-25 sub-pod, paid an unexpected and unusual visit to Dyes Inlet, a small estuary in Puget Sound, near Seattle, Washington. Most experts believe they were following a run of chum salmon or maybe they were just curious, as killer whales can be. Either way, their thirty-day visit was unforgettable for anyone who had the chance to observe these highly social animals up close.

When I decided I wanted to create a story to share the special excitement of that experience almost twenty years ago, I read all I could about the actual event, spoke to whale researchers, journalists, and community residents, and visited Dyes Inlet many times. Much of what I learned became part of this book.

But as fiction authors often do, I took some liberties in my story, adjusting timelines, changing settings, and creating a slantwise version of the geography of the inlet. In this book, SoundKeeper is loosely based on the Soundwatch Boater Education Program at the Whale Museum in Friday Harbor, Washington (www.whalemuseum.org) who work to prevent vessel disturbance to killer whales and other marine wildlife in the Salish Sea. While the pod genealogy chart shows the actual whales that visited Dyes Inlet, some small details have been changed. For example, in real life Muncher is a girl!

When I finished my research and began writing, something interesting happened. My story moved beyond a retelling of the specifics of the actual event. Other themes and connections began to emerge, and the mystery of why the whales stayed in the inlet for so long became much more central. To me, that is the beauty of storytelling. The factual events of the orcas visit became the framework for a story that explores loss, courage, faith, and what it means to call a place home.

J, K, and L pods still frequent the inland waterways of Washington State and the boundary waters between the United States and Canada every spring through fall. In the winter months, they have been spotted as far south as central California.

Their numbers declined sharply in the late 1960s as a result of live captures of killer whales for aquarium displays, including the infamous Penn Cove capture in August 1970 that Marisa learns about from Tal and Kevin. In 2005, the Southern Residents were placed on the Endangered Species List, mostly due to its small population size. As of December 31, 2015, J, K, and L pods numbers totaled eighty-four.[1]

Lolita, one of the whales taken at Penn Cove, is the last surviving orca of forty-five members of the Southern Resident community that was captured. On February 4, 2015, Lolita was officially included in the endangered listing of the Southern Residents. For

[1] Center for Whale Research

years, Orca Network (www.orcanetwork.org) has been working tirelessly to bring Lolita back to the Northwest, where her retirement home awaits.

So if you find yourself falling in love with orcas, or you'd just like to learn more about the SRKW, a great resource is the Center for Whale Research (www.whaleresearch.com) in Friday Harbor. To hear what the whales sound like when they're communicating to each other, try listening in on the Salish Sea Hydrophone Network (www.orcasound.net) or at Listening for Orcas (www.listen.orcasound.net).

Finally, the Suquamish Museum (www.suquamishmuseum.org) is a great place to learn more about the history and vibrant culture of this Coast Salish tribe and their ancestral leader Chief Seattle, whose ideas on personal values and environmental responsibility remain important today.

As you read and learn more about the ways of the orcas, my wish for all my readers is that, like Marisa, each of you discovers your own passion in life, whatever that may be, and you find the courage and faith within yourself to follow it as it calls you home.

ACKNOWLEDGMENTS

My deepest thanks to . . .

~ All the many people who worked long and hard at WestWinds Press, making this a stronger book, but especially my talented and perceptive editor Michelle McCann and publisher Douglas Pfeiffer, who believed in this story from the beginning.

~ My writing community at the Whidbey Writers Workshop MFA program and SCBWI-Western Washington, many of whom read some or all of this manuscript at various stages and offered wise and perceptive criticism: Bonny Becker, Kirby Larson, Carmen Bernier-Grand, Wayne Ude, Ann Gonzalez, Stephanie Lile, Kobbie Alamo, Grier Jewell, Frances Wood, and Annie Boochever. Thanks also to Evelyn Fazio who shared insights on story structure and characters.

~ Mary Ruckelshaus, formerly of NOAA's Northwest Fisheries Science Center and Kelly Balcomb-Bartok of the Center for Whale Research who read early drafts of this manuscript and offered valuable advice and expertise on marine ecosystems and the ways of killer whales. Any and all errors that remain are mine alone.

~ Susan Berta and Howard Garrett of Orca Network who helped me envision the enormity of the Penn Cove orca captures and the circumstances of Lolita's past, present, and future.

~ The staff at Soundwatch Boater Education, a program of the Whale Museum in Friday Harbor, Washington, who answered any and all my questions related to boating, marine laws, and the impact of marine traffic on the Southern Resident killer whales.

~ Lydia Sigo, Curator/Archivist at the Suquamish Museum, for her understanding, support, and generosity of spirit in addition to practical guidance on the Puget Sound Coast Salish tribes.

~ Peg Deam of the Suquamish Tribe and Michele Balagot of the Tulalip Tribes, Lushootseed Department, who helped with translation and recorded specific words so I could hear spoken Lushootseed.

I gleaned a wealth of information and perspective on the ways of whales from the extensive work being done on behalf of orca conservation at the Center for Whale Research in Friday Harbor and Orca Conservancy in Seattle, as well as real-time underwater sound recordings of orca vocalizations available through the Salish Sea Hydrophone Network. Newspaper reports from 1997 and the ten-year anniversary compilation published in the Kitsap Sun provided invaluable, up-close and personal details to L-25's visit to Dyes Inlet. Two excellent books also provided additional history and context on *Orcinus orca*: Alexandra Morton's *Listening to Whales: What the Orcas Have Taught Us* and David Neiwert's *Of Orcas and Men: What Killer Whales Can Teach Us*.

Closer to home, my thanks to Sue Williams Judge, who helped me understand nursing, emergency care, and the complex issues involved in adoption and helping families in crisis; Jim Hill and family for their Pasadena stories; Charlie Taffett for letting me borrow his name; and Etsuko Koh, owner of Fresh Flours Pastries in Seattle, where much of this book was written. Every hour spent in her shop, I was made to feel welcome.

And finally, to Carol Mentyka, Mark Phillips and Megan Corwin, Karen Hirsch, Marilyn Davie, Barbara Young, Kevin Johnston and Betsy Whitaker, Joe and Trudi Picciano, James Ferraro, and Michael Poling, who listened, counseled, supported, and encouraged me every step of the way—you have my boundless gratitude.

Especially and always, to Stephen and Lena, thank you for taking that leap of faith with me.

CHASING AT THE SURFACE

Discussion Questions

1. Lena and Marisa are best friends but they react very differently to the events and problems they face in this book. What are some differences you noticed? Does this strengthen or weaken their friendship? What are some ways that each girl expresses her friendship for the other?

2. Why do you think Marisa refuses to read Mom's letters? Do you think this decision helps her to better deal with Mom leaving or does it make it worse? Would you make the same decision if you were in a similar situation?

3. When Mom leaves home, Marisa and Dad don't know where she's going or why. Do you think this was the right thing for Mom to do? Why do you think she made that decision? Can you think of other ways she could have handled it?

4. How does Marisa feel when she learns that Muncher, the little orca calf she and Mom adopted, is in the inlet? Why do you think she has these feelings?

5. In the beginning, Marisa says that she and Dad both "let Mom go without a fight." Do you think that the whales' visit helped Marisa learn to fight for what she wants? How? Is there a particular point in the story where you see this change happening?

6. At different times in the story Harris and Marisa both take a boat out on the inlet and find themselves in danger. What is similar about the two events and what is different? Do you think the decision each character made was good or bad?

7. What does Harris mean when he tells Marisa that her mother "got it"? Why does this shock and upset Marisa so much?

8. When the whales first come into the inlet, everyone is excited, but the longer they stay things begin to change. What changes did you notice? Why do you think this is? How do you think you would have behaved if you were there watching when the whales arrived?

9. Marisa knows a lot about orcas and she learns even more from the whale researchers who come to visit from Friday Harbor. What are some things you learned from this book about whales that you didn't know before? Do you feel differently about orca whales and the environment they live in after reading this book?

10. At the community meeting, what does Kevin mean when he says that the herding of the whales on the inlet was like "Penn Cove without the net"?

11. Do you think it was right that people used to capture whales to put them on display in aquariums? Why or why not? What specific examples in the book made you feel the way you do?

12. Why do you think Bette and Tal give Marisa their daughter Carol Ann's charm bracelet? Do you think Carol Ann would be okay with this if she knew?

13. What discovery does Marisa make that helps her solve the mystery of why the whales won't leave the inlet? What clues earlier in the story foreshadow this discovery?

14. What does Marisa learn from the culture of the Coast Salish tribes during the time of the whales' visit? How does this help her get the whales home?

15. Two main themes of this book are finding courage to fight for what you believe in and the meaning of family. How do Harris and Marisa differ in their views on these two themes? Do their ideas change from the start of the book to the end? Are there other characters/people in the book who also demonstrate the meaning of family?

16. What do you think the first meeting will be like between Marisa and her half-brother, Ben? How are they different and what do they have in common? What can each of them teach the other?

17. Whales are very intelligent animals, but as Naomi tells Marisa, there is still a lot that scientists don't know about them. Do you think some of the communication and interaction that Marisa and her friends have with L-Pod could really happen? Which parts seem most realistic and which might be just Marisa's imagination? Does it make a difference to the decisions Marisa ultimately makes to help the whales?

18. There are many instances in the book that talk about whales and salmon. What have you learned about the connections between orca whales and salmon after reading this book? Can you think of other animal relationships like this that also exist?

19. Did it make a difference to you to know that the story was partially based on a real-life incident? Why or why not?

20. Why do you think the author titled the book "Chasing at the Surface"?

CPSIA information can be obtained at www.ICGtesting.com
Printed in the USA
BVOW06s0456111016

464702BV00005B/10/P